4/23

Praise for OTHER WORDS FOR HOME

John Newbery Medal Honor Book

Walter Dean Myers Award for Outstanding Children's Literature Honor Book, Younger Readers

Lee Bennett Hopkins Poetry Honor

NCTE Charlotte Huck Award for Outstanding Fiction for Children Honor Book

Middle East Book Award by the Middle East Outreach Council, Youth Literature Winner

Cybils Awards Finalist, Poetry

Honorable Mention Arab American Book Award, Children/Young Adult

Friends of American Writers Young People's Literature Award Winner

Nautilus Book Award Silver Winner, Middle Grade Fiction

Goodreads Choice Award Nominee, Middle Grade

Junior Library Guild Selection

ALSC Notable Book

Top 10 Indie Next List Pick

Ohioana Library Youth Literature Award

NPR's Favorite Books

Kirkus Reviews Best Middle Grade Books in Verse

Publishers Weekly Best Middle Grade Books

School Library Journal Best Middle Grade Books

ALA *Booklist* Editor's Choice

Center fo   Literature Best Book of the Year

"In this timely book rhythmic lines distill Jude's deepest emotions. Warga effectively shows, as she writes in an author's note, that 'children who are fleeing from a war zone . . . want the same things all of us do—love, understanding, safety, a chance at happiness.'" —*Publishers Weekly* (starred review)

"Warga portrays with extraordinary talent the transformation of a family's life before and after the war began in Syria. Her free-verse narration cuts straight to the bone [and] confronts the difficult realities of being Muslim and Arab in the US. Poetic, immersive, hopeful." —*Kirkus Reviews* (starred review)

"Warga's middle-grade debut puts its hands around your heart and holds it, ever so gently, so that you're aware of your own fragility and resilience: just as Jude is while her life changes drastically. *Other Words for Home* should find its way into every middle-grade reader's hands." —ALA *Booklist* (starred review)

"This powerful middle grade novel explores the complicated concepts of war and corruption, home, family, [and] belonging. Highly recommended for all libraries." —*School Library Journal* (starred review)

"Convincing and authentic, infused with thoughtfulness, humor, determination, and hope. A realistic portrait of the strength it takes to move to a new country, as well as of the complicated dynamics between first- and second-generation immigrants." —*The Horn Book* (starred review)

"Warga situates her verse novel at a sweet spot for middle-graders. The complications of assessing whether Jude is as lucky as everyone makes her out to be ring poignantly true, and when Jude takes her place on the school stage, Warga's audience will surely applaud." —*The Bulletin of the Center for Children's Books*

"Poetic and powerful. There are so many reasons to read this novel. It's a book about kindness, for one; it sings, for another. And that's Jude. I wanted nothing more than to be her friend and listen to whatever she had to say about life. She deserves to shine in the spotlight, and so does *Other Words for Home*."—NPR

"Through Jude's eyes readers see firsthand what it is to leave behind one's beloved home and family as many refugees do every single day. Young readers will laugh with Jude, cry with her, and root for her every step of the way. A beautiful, powerful, and necessary book for all readers." —Aisha Saeed, *New York Times* bestselling author of *Amal Unbound*

"*Other Words for Home* is a salve for the world we live in today. It's a hope-filled story that doesn't pander but instead peels back layers of culture and identity, fear and prejudice, exile and belonging, all wrapped around a young Syrian girl—Jude. Chocked with equal parts fear and moxie, Jude is a heart trying to figure out how to beat outside the body. I ached for, but simultaneously found that though our stories are different, I am her. This is a necessary story. We're lucky to have it in the world." —Jason Reynolds, award-winning, bestselling author of *Ghost* and *Long Way Down*

"An emotional, gorgeous book that takes you into the fraught interior life of Jude, a dreamer, actress, daughter and little sister—who is also a Syrian refugee. Jude's story is one that is rarely shared, which makes its relatability that much more powerful. An absolute must-read book." —Sabaa Tahir, #1 *New York Times* bestselling author of the Ember in the Ashes series

OTHER WORDS for Home

JASMINE WARGA

BALZER + BRAY

An Imprint of HarperCollins*Publishers*

Library of Congress Control Number: 2018961861
ISBN 978-0-06-274781-5

Typography by Jenna Stempel-Lobell
22 23 24 25   PC/BRR   11

First paperback edition, 2021

This one's for the Nazeks,
especially my father, who crossed an ocean,
my uncle Abdalla, who loved me from across one,
and my cousin Jude, whose name I borrowed.

PART ONE
Changing

I.

It is almost summer and everywhere smells like fish,
    except for right down by the sea
    where if you hold your nose just right
    you can smell the sprawling jasmine and the salt water
    instead.

In the summer, I always hold my nose to avoid
    the stench of fish and
    tourists that smell like hairspray
    and money and French perfume.
    The tourists come from Damascus and Aleppo.
    Sometimes even Beirut and Amman.
    Once I met a man all the way from Doha.
    I asked him about the big skyscrapers that I have heard
    reach all the way up to the heavens,
    but Baba hushed me quiet before the man could
        answer me.

Baba does not like for me to talk to
Tourists

Strangers
Men.

He does not want me to talk to anyone that I do not
      know
and even people that I do know he always says,
Jude, skety,
and so I bite my tongue and it sometimes tastes even
      worse
than the way the summer fish smell.

Everyone is saying that there will be fewer visitors
from Aleppo this year.
That there is no one left in Aleppo to come.
That everyone who could leave Aleppo already has.
When I ask Mama if this is true, she says,
Jude, skety.

II.

Our city does not look like what they show on TV of Syria.
    I remember the first time
    Fatima and I saw a story
    about Aleppo on the news.
    We felt proud.

    I know that is strange to say, childish maybe—
    it felt strange even then—
    but it also felt like the rest of the world
    saw
    me.

    But our city does not look like Aleppo, before or after.
    It is not sprawling and noisy with buildings
    pressed up against
    one another
    like they are crammed together in an elevator
    with no room to breathe.

    Our city is on the sea. It sits below the mountains.
    It is where the rest of Syria comes when they want to

breathe.

No one is going to come this year, Fatima says.

And I wonder if that is because there is no one left
who needs to
breathe.

III.

Fatima is twenty-four days, six hours, and eleven minutes
older than me.
　　She did the math.
　　Fatima hates math, but loves
　　when she comes out on
　　top.

　　We have always been friends.
　　Mama and Aunt Amal have known each other
　　since they were girls.
　　We live across the courtyard from them and
　　sometimes when I was little,
　　I would squeeze my eyes shut at night and
　　pretend that Fatima and I
　　were dreaming the same dream.

　　When I was little, it was easy to imagine that.
　　Fatima and I were always in step,
　　four feet pointed in the same direction.

But the last few months have been different.
Fatima feels kilometers ahead of me now.
Her dark curls aren't on display anymore,
tumbling to her shoulders
in unruly waves that remind me of laughter.
Her head is wrapped in silk scarves
that are bright and colored like jewels.

She is one of the first girls in our grade to cover.
She has bled between her legs.

I am still waiting
to bleed.
To feel like I have something worth
covering.

IV.

Fatima and I almost always have our *asroneyeh* together.
    Either Mama makes it or Auntie Amal.
    Fatima likes to have olives, green and black,
    so fat that you can stick your fingers inside of them
    and eat them one by one.

    I think olives taste like the sea
    and all that salt makes me dizzy.
    I eat the *jebneh* and the bread
    that Mama gets from Hibah's bakery
    around the corner
    because she knows it is my favorite.
    Hibah makes her bread as fluffy as a pillow.

    I eat so much of it that Mama
    always has to remind me that
    asroneyeh is supposed to help me last until dinner,
    but is not dinner.

    During *asroneyeh*, we drink tea.

Or Fatima drinks tea and I drink sugar and mint
with a side of tea.

We watch old American movies that we bought
with our Eid and birthday money.
We watch Julia Roberts fall in love and
we watch Sandra Bullock track down criminals and
we watch Reese Witherspoon go to law school.

Fatima and I both want to be movie stars.
Fatima also wants to be a doctor,
but I only want to be a
movie star.

The wanting pulses so hard in my chest that it
        sometimes hurts.

My older brother, Issa,
used to watch the movies with us.
He would sometimes even act them out with us,
standing up on the couch,
imitating Reese's way of speaking English,
all slow and sugary.

He used to until one day Baba came home from work
        early and walked in on us
acting out the movies. Baba didn't say anything.

Not even *Jude, skety.*
He didn't even look at me.
Only at Issa.
He shook his head
and walked into his bedroom.

V.

Fatima and I like to find bits
    and pieces of ourselves in the faces of
    movie stars.

    We have decided that Fatima has Sandra Bullock's
    dark eyes that are so expressive you could tell
    if she was laughing
    even if her mouth was covered.

    Speaking of mouths, I have one.
    And it is big
    like Julia Roberts's.
    At least that's what I tell myself.

    Someday
    I hope I will be a movie star
    and some other little girl will look at me and say
    I have her eyes
    her nose
    her hair

her laugh
and she will feel beautiful.

Maybe
someday
Julia Roberts will see me and think
I have her mouth.

VI.

I am walking down by the shore
 with my favorite person in the whole world,
 my older brother, Issa.

 We are strolling down the stretch of beach
 that is open to everyone.
 Only people who—like Issa and me—have always
  lived here
 walk on this beach.
 Only people who don't have piles and piles of money
 walk on this beach.

 Soon, we will be able to walk anywhere we want, Issa says.
 Things are going to change.
 I follow his eyes to the other side of the beach
 where there are plush white chairs
 shaded by white-and-blue-striped canopies.
 The chairs sit empty,
 but they are not open.
 The salty wind is whipping through Issa's dark hair
 and he is wearing his serious face.

His serious face is new.
Issa used to love to sing American pop songs
with me and Fatima
at the top of his lungs.
He knew every word of
Madonna
Whitney Houston
Mariah Carey.

Now he knows other words like
revolution
democracy
and change, change, change.
He is always talking about *change*.

My feet sink into the sand
and I realize I do not want things to change.
I want things to go back to the way they were,
which I guess is another sort of changing,
but it is not what Issa is talking about.

The sky is melting overhead.
The sun, like my feet, is sinking
lower and
lower,
swirls of yellows and dusty pinks.

Are you coming to dinner?

It still feels strange to ask my brother this question.
His presence at *ghadah* used to be as certain as the
     sunset,
but now that has also
changed.

Issa's face switches again,
from serious to sorry,
and I know he isn't coming.

I'm meeting Saeed and Yasmine, he says,
and Baba would tell you that my brother
and his friends
are plotting revolution.

Our baba is furious that Issa goes
to these meetings.
He calls them treasonous and
Issa says that it is our president
Bashar al-Assad
who is treasonous,
who is oppressing his own people.

Issa shouts at Baba about free elections
and real democracy
and unlawful use of force
and Baba shouts about stability
and safety and then stability again.

You should come with me, Issa says,
bringing me out of my memory
and back to the beach.

He knows that I can't.
I am not like Issa.
I am good at taking an extra piece of bread at *ghadah*,
at talking too loud and too quickly
about American movie stars.
I am not good at defying Baba.

You should care about our country, too, he says.

I do, I say,
but what I mean is that I care
about my brother
and my baba
and my mama
and I just want to live in a country where
we can all have dinner again
without shouting about our president
or rebels and revolution.

VII.

Last summer
    Fatima and I met a girl who was from Damascus.
    Her name was Samira
    but she told us to call her Sammy
    which was what her friend from London called her.

    London, she said.
    Did we know where that was?
    We said yes, which was true
    and not true.
    I've heard of London but
    I wouldn't know how to get there.

    Sammy pronounced the word *London*
    like Mary Poppins does in the movie and
    I almost laughed but
    then I realized she wasn't trying to be funny.
    She was being *posh,*
    which is an English word she taught me.

Sammy's family had lots of money.
She was staying at the hotel right by the sea
that has the fancy white chairs that are shaded
with fancy white canopies.

The kind of hotel that Issa hates,
but I secretly like and dream about staying at one day.
I picture myself as a famous actress,
coming home to visit,
sitting on one of those fancy white chairs,
reading a glossy magazine with my face on the cover.

VIII.

The hotel where Sammy was staying is right around the
corner
    from Baba's store
    where he sells candy bars
    and soft drinks and magazines to the tourists.
    His prices are much better than at the shops in the
        fancy hotels.

    Sammy was picking out a candy bar when
    she heard Fatima and me talking
    near the back of the store.

    Fatima and I like to hang out at Baba's store.
    Sometimes he gives us free Fanta
    sometimes free chips
    and there are always interesting people coming
    and going
    especially in the summer.

    If we don't cause too much trouble

Baba lets us hang around.
He would never admit it but I think he actually likes
when we come to visit him.

You like American movies? Sammy said to us
in English.
She'd heard Fatima and me talking so I knew
she spoke Arabic,
but she wanted us to know she also spoke
English.
Yes, Fatima said loudly back to her
in English,
even though Fatima's accent is not as good as mine.

Baba gave us a warning glance
from behind the counter,
and we all slunk further down the aisle,
hiding behind the Kit Kats and the M&M's.

Which films do you like? she asked,
again in English.
Fatima looked to me.
My English has always been better than hers.

Miss Congeniality.
Runaway Bride.
Legally Blonde.

Practical Magic.
Pretty Woman.

The last two we weren't supposed to watch
because witches
and prostitutes scare
Mama and Auntie Amal
but Issa bought us those movies
from a store in our neighborhood that sells recordings
of American movies.
We hid the tapes in a box
behind a pile of clothes that I don't wear anymore.

Sammy frowned at us.
Later I would realize this was the moment she decided
Fatima and I
were not posh.

You like old movies.
We gave her a blank stare and she said,
What about . . . ?
She listed lots of movie titles we had never heard of.

Later that summer, Sammy took Fatima and me
to the movie theater that is right downtown
by the fancy new shops
that were built just for the tourists.

Fatima and I had never been to that movie theater
or any movie theater and
we tried to pretend not to be stunned by the
soft red velvet seats that are so dense you can make
a handprint in the fabric
or the wide flat white screen
that is larger than anything
I'd ever seen.

We watched a new American movie
and I didn't recognize any of the movie stars.
They talked so fast and I spent most of the time
trying to keep up with the subtitles that rolled across
the bottom of the screen.

Afterward, Sammy said,
See, now you will be able to talk about a movie
that isn't a hundred years old.
I smiled and didn't tell Sammy that I still liked
Miss Congeniality
better.

IX.

Today the air is so soupy
　　that it feels like I am living inside
　　someone else's mouth.
　　I wake up at the sound of the first *adhan*,
　　the muezzin's voice echoing through my room.
　　But I do not get up to pray.
　　Instead I roll over and press my face
　　into my pillow and
　　pray for cool air
　　and sleep.

　　When I get up, Mama is in the kitchen brewing tea.
　　She has set out large chunks of feta
　　and slightly toasted pitas.
　　She toasts them right on the open flame in our kitchen.
　　I know that everyone's mother makes them this way,
　　but I still cannot imagine doing it
　　myself one day.

　　It seems so bold.

So brave.
It is playing with fire.

Baba has already left for work.
In the summer, his store has extended hours.
In the summer, he is a ghost that I do not see.
I only know he exists by the footsteps I hear
in the early mornings and late evenings.

Mama is telling Issa to eat.
She is telling him not to go to the march
that is planned for today.

Life is good.
We should not tempt fate,
Mama says.

Life is not good for everyone.
You only think it is good because that is
what you have been told.
You need to
open your eyes,
Issa says.

I stretch my eyes as wide as I can.
I want him to laugh,
but he just

shakes his head.
I used to be able to make him laugh,
but not anymore.
I have not heard him laugh in
ages.

We live in a town where most people do not speak ill
of our president.
But my brother does.
So do his friends who
attend the local university.
They have ideas about how the world should be.

Issa says he wants to live in a country where
anyone can be
anyone
they want to be.

I don't understand what my brother means
when he says this.
I wish I understood exactly what my brother
wants to be.

Our president's family grew up
in the mountains to the north of us,
and if you listen carefully you can hear
the whispers rolling down the mountains,

telling us to stay quiet
and be grateful.
The president's ancestors are
powerful spirits.

We live in a town that needs tourists.
Revolution
and war are not good
for business.

But my brother doesn't care.
My brother who no longer will
imitate Reese Witherspoon
or sing Whitney Houston
with me.

My brother wants to see things change,
and I just want to hear him laugh
again.

X.

Mama forbids me to leave our apartment
    on the day of the protest.
    She tries to forbid Issa,
    but, of course, he does not
    listen.

I sit on the couch by the small window
and look out into the courtyard.
It is as quiet as
always.

Maybe even more quiet. The two benches are
empty.
The one potted plant of mint has grown out of control.
It smells like strong tea
and is spilling out of its container,
taking over everything around it.

No one knows how the mint got there;
someone should do something about that.

But everyone is waiting
for someone else to do it.

We are still waiting.

I stare at the window of Fatima's apartment.
I keep thinking I will see her, sitting by the glass,
listening, watching, and waiting.
Just like me.

But I don't see her.

I pace back
and forth by the window.
Sometimes I think I can hear the protests.
I stretch my ears for miles
and miles,
itching to catch a sound of the angry students
with their signs.

Imagining my brother's face,
red and angry.
Chanting about freedom and democracy,
words that I know, but don't quite
understand.

I know my brother is shouting for

his country.
But I also feel like he is shouting at Baba.

I do not think Baba is
listening.

XI.

I am sitting next to Baba at his store.
    He has never told me that he likes when I visit,
    but I think he does because
    whenever I come,
    there is always another stool,
    sitting next to his,
    empty,
    waiting.

    Today is a good day because
    Baba is letting me eat a candy bar
    from his shop.
    I am trying to eat it slowly,
    to savor it.
    But instead I eat it all
    in four quick bites.

    Is this what your brother wants?

    My head jerks up,
    surprised by the sound of my father's voice,

31

surprised he is asking
me
a question.

He hands me a newspaper.
The front page is filled with awful pictures of
people who are
bloodied and cowering together in their city,
which has been torn apart by war.

He wants these violent maniacs to take over?
My father shoves the paper closer to me.
I do not touch the paper.
I avoid it like a hot plate that will burn me.

I look away from the pictures.
I don't want to see them.
I don't want to think about them later tonight
when I am trying to fall asleep.

I know that Issa and his friends are different from
    those men.
Those men who spill blood and manipulate the Quran
    to say
things that the rest of us know it does not say.

Baba has to know that too,

and I move my lips to tell him,
but cannot make myself say the words.
I am not brave like my brother.

Take it, he says,
and he is no longer asking me.
I hold the newspaper in my hands
and it feels heavy for something made only of paper.

You can keep it. If your brother has his way
there will be no one left in this town
who can afford to buy a paper anymore anyway.

I clutch the newspaper,
wishing that he had given me a different gift,
like another candy bar.

XII.

After the protests,
    there are more police.
    It seems like everywhere you go—
    the butcher
    the beach
    at school—
    there is an armed policeman.

    There are whispers of people
    who were rounded up after the protests
    and locked in jail.

    There are louder whispers about a town nearby
    where men with stolen tanks and stolen weapons
    rolled in and took over.

    Those men are now fighting
    against the government's army
    and the people who live in the town
    don't know whose side to choose.
    They only want the violence to stop.

Nobody knows which side is the right one anymore.
When I go with Mama to the spice shop
to refill her containers of coriander and za'atar,
Mama makes a big show out of bowing her head
in the direction of the framed portrait of our president.

But when we get home
and she is spreading the spice rub over the lamb legs,
she talks to my brother
who is finally home for a dinner.

I know this is not what you expected, she says.
Her hands massage the meat.
The whole kitchen fills with the earthy scent of herbs.
You were not wrong to want better.

Issa sits at the table.
He is having an *asroneyeh*
to hold him over until dinner is ready.
He rips a piece of pita bread in half.
I know, he says,
and his eyes meet mine.
An invitation.
A dare.
I am not going to stop wanting better.

He rips the bread into
smaller

and smaller pieces.
This is not the end.
It is only the beginning.

XIII.

Our town used to be
    a place for people to laugh and enjoy
    all the things that unite them like
    family and sunshine and the sea and good food.
    Not the things that divide them like
    opinions and political loyalties.

    But now everyone wants to know
    where you stand.
    What you think.
    What you believe.

    When you walk around town,
    you had better show deference to our president—
    to his large picture that is in almost every shop,
    and the armed guards that are now on every corner.

    If you don't,
    you will be asked if you would rather
    live in one of those other towns,
    towns that are no longer under our president's control.

Towns where families huddle together in rubble,
and there is no running water and electricity,
but a whole lot of blood.

I still smile at everyone in the street.
Not everyone smiles back, though.
When they don't,
I want to say,
You don't have to worry about me.
I am just a girl who likes movies.

XIV.

At first when my brother moves out,
    I am forbidden from going to his new apartment.

Children are not supposed to move out until they've finished
        university, Mama says
as she folds the shirts that Issa left behind,
neatly leaving them in his drawer,
like she is preparing for him to move back in
    tomorrow.

Baba, as expected, does not say anything
about my brother moving out.
But I catch him glancing
in the direction of my brother's
now empty room
when he doesn't think anyone is watching.

I ask every day if I can visit my brother,
and every day the answer is no,
until one day when my mama says

yes and she walks with me the seven blocks across town
    to his new apartment,
which is near the local university
and all of the cafés that Baba thinks are full of radicals.

Mama does not go inside,
but I see her lingering outside
watching me climb down the steps
into the basement where my brother now lives,
into an entirely new world.

His new apartment is covered with a tapestry of
    mismatched rugs;
a scratched coffee table sits low to the ground
and it is covered with stacks of newspapers that have
    been marked up with a pen.
Names have been circled, crossed out, and amended.

It feels like a place where ideas live.
There is an energy in the room that excites
and frightens me.

There are so many faces,
girls and boys.
Issa introduces me to everyone.
I do not know which faces actually live in this place
and which faces are only visiting,
like me.

XV.

There is a loud knock at the door,
    and soon my brother's basement apartment is filled
      with armed police.
There is shouting,
glasses knocked to the ground,
bodies shoved against walls,
the sounds of handcuffs clicking,
more shouting.

In the chaos,
my brother reaches for my hand.
He pulls me with him,
down a hallway,
up a flight of stairs,
out a door.

When we are outside,
I let out one long gasp.
Don't be afraid, Jude, he says.
I wouldn't let anything happen to you.

But my knees won't stop shaking.
They could have taken you, I say, my voice trembling.

He squeezes my hand again.
It feels like some sort of promise,
an assurance that he won't leave me
all alone.

XVI.

Mama knows what happened
    before Issa even brings me home.

    She clings to both of us
    and makes a sound I have never heard before.
    It sounds like terror,
    like primal relief.

    They could have taken you, she says,
    still squeezing us both tightly.
    It is exactly what I said to Issa.

    There is an Arabic proverb that says:
    The offspring of ducks float.
    It means,
    all children end up like their parents.
    I guess I am starting
    to float.

XVII.

After the raid on Issa's apartment,
    My mama, who has never been afraid of anything,
    suddenly is squeezing my hand tight
    when we walk to the market,
    pulling me close to her at every corner,
    looking ten times before we cross the street.

    I watch her when she makes dinner.
    She does everything a little slower
    than she used to.
    It's like there is now a blinking caution light
    inside of her.

    Even Baba checks the lock
    on the door
    twice every night,
    rubs Mama's shoulders more than he used to,
    though I'm not sure if that's to make her
    or him
    feel better.
    Maybe both.

I hear them late at night,
whispering back and forth to one another.
I can't always make out the actual words,
but I can feel them,
taste them.

They taste like fear.

I stare up at the ceiling of my room.
I wonder where my brother is,
if he's staring up at his ceiling,
in his new apartment,
if he's afraid like me,
if he's afraid at all.

XVIII.

When Mama first tells me,
 it's just us
 sitting at the kitchen table,
 sharing a snack of feta cheese and olives.

 It's only a visit, she says,
 to see my brother.

 My heart drops into my stomach.
 Her brother lives an ocean away
 in America.

 We have never visited him because
 it is not an easy place to visit.
 It is a long trip.
 An expensive one.
 It is not a trip you would take for no reason.

 We are leaving, I challenge her.
 I look in her eyes
 demanding she tell me the truth.

Sunlight streams in through the cracks in the blinds.
She used to leave our windows all the way open during
     the day.

Only for a little while, she admits,
and I can tell she wants to believe
what she is saying.
She wants to believe it for both of us.

What about Baba? I ask and watch
Mama's big dark eyes fill up with tears.
What about Issa?
The tears spill over.

She tells me that Baba has to stay because he cannot
will not
leave the store.
She tells me that Issa
will not
leave.

I wish he would, she says,
holding out her hand to me,
and I know she means it to be comforting
that we both wish this,
but it only makes my heart hurt more.

Why do we have to go?

Her eyes are still wet.
She squeezes my hand tighter.
I'm sorry, habibti, but I cannot wait for things to get worse.
We cannot take the risk.

But things might not get worse, I argue.
I am thinking of everything I heard that night
in Issa's basement.
Ideas about hope
and freedom.

Mama puts her hand on her stomach.
Jude, she says. *I need you.*

I need you, she repeats.
To help us.

My eyes study her hand,
her belly,
the rise and fall of her breath.

And all of a sudden,
I see all the pieces and how they fit.
My eyes are still watery, but I smile.

A baby? I say because I am worried
that if it's not said out loud
it won't be true.

Nunu, she confirms.
I slide out of my chair
and snuggle up to her belly,
pressing my ear against the soft fabric of her dress,
and I swear I hear
a heartbeat.

I am learning how to be
sad
and happy
at the same time.

XIX.

It is our last day
and I am supposed to be packing.

Fatima and Auntie Amal have come over
to say good-bye.
I wanted to have a big party but
Mama said no.

She says there is no need
to make a big fuss
when we will be back soon

but the way she says *soon*
with the click of her tongue
makes it sound like a wish
instead of the truth.

Even though we aren't having a big party
Auntie Amal still brought me sweets
from Chez Mariana

which is my favorite bakery.
Mariana went to Paris to study
and her bakery is filled with
tarts stuffed full of rich creams and
cakes that look like they belong in a fashion magazine.

Mama says that only tourists would pay
Mariana's prices for cake.
Mama says the word *cake* like it's just an ordinary food,
which is strange since everyone knows that cakes are
    made of magic.

I am on my second slice of cake
my hands sticky with the vanilla bean icing
when Fatima says,
You won't forget me, will you?

I laugh and my knees go
weak so I sit on the floor
but Fatima swats at me.

Don't laugh, she says and her voice cracks,
thick with emotion,
driving a rushing river between us,
with her on one side
and me on the other bank.
I want to swim back toward her,

but for the first time ever,
I'm not sure how.

When I look into her movie star–like eyes
I see real worry.
I couldn't forget you even if I wanted to.
Fatima gives me her Take Me Seriously face.
She always wants me to be serious.
She likes dramas where people
fall in
and out of
and into love.
Where they
cry and sigh and cry some more.

I like comedies where people
laugh and then laugh
some more.

No one ever tells people in comedies to
grow up.

Fatima walks over to my bed
and sticks her head in one of the boxes
that I haven't sorted yet.

She picks up two scarves,

one for each fist,
and waves them like she is
at the finish line of a race.

Are you going to bring these?
What she wants to ask is,
Are you going to wear these in America?
Are you going to grow up without me?

I take the scarves from her,
one
by one
and neatly place them in the
one bag
Mama has given me to pack up my
whole
life.

What would you like to eat?
she asks me, in English,
and we both laugh.
How are you doing today? she says,
a broad smile on her face.

For years now,
we have practiced English phrases.
I wonder if speaking English in America

will be anything like speaking English here at school.
I wonder if anything about America will be like it is
here.

I'll write to you every day, I say.
Promise?
I nod and the river that rushed between us before
begins to dry up
and even though I am leaving
and she is staying,
it feels like we're standing on the same shore again.

XX.

When I say good-bye to Baba,
    he hugs me tight,
    his arms saying everything that his lips don't.

    His tight embrace tells me to
    be good and
    listen to Mama.

    His tight embrace tells me that
    he is going to miss us
    a lot.

    My brother has come over to say good-bye, too.
    It is all four,
    five, my mind corrects,
    of us in the same room and I wonder when,
    if,
    it will ever be like this again.

    Issa picks me up off the ground
    and twirls me around.

When he sets me back down,
he gives me a wide smile.
The type of smile I haven't seen on his face
in a very long time.
The type of smile he used to wear
when we would spend hours
reciting movies and singing along to
Madonna and Whitney.

I don't understand how you can be so happy, I say.
I'm leaving.
I say the second part in case my brother forgot
because recently,
he's been forgetting a lot of things,
to come home for dinner,
to pick up the phone when we call,
to let us know that he's okay.

I see Issa's smile falter a little
and somehow this makes me happy,
a little.

Aren't you going to miss me? I ask.
He pulls me close,
and whispers, *Akeed.*
But you're going to have so much fun in America.
It's going to be an adventure.

He must be able to tell I'm about to argue with him
Because he kisses the top of my head.
Then he brings his face close to mine
and whispers in my ear,
Be brave.

My knees lock and I am about to tell him
I don't know how to do that.
But then I see Baba embracing Mama.
He is gently patting her stomach
and I have never seen Baba look so
proud and so worried all at the same time.

And that's when I realize I don't have a choice.
I'm going to have to learn how to be brave.

We're all going to have to learn.

PART TWO
Arriving

I.

The plane flight is
  long.

    Our seats are near the back of the plane,
    Mama pressed against the window and me
    pressed against her.

    While Mama sleeps,
    I look out the window.
    When the sun rises,
    I can see the ground below.

    It all looks so
    tiny
    and far away.

    I gasp but no one
    hears me.

II.

From the window of the plane,
    I see a muddy river
    framed by green rolling hills
    that are dotted with houses.
    I wonder which of those houses will now be mine.

We arrive,
in a city that I cannot pronounce,
a city called Cincinnati.

When the plane lands,
Mama and I are quickly directed to a long line
for people like us,
people who are not from America,
but who are trying to enter.

The line moves slowly.
My eyelids feel heavy
and my body does not have any idea what time it is.

It is finally our turn.
We are called up to talk with a man
sitting in a booth
under a sign that says
immigration.

The man beckons for us to step up closer.
He has kind blue eyes that seem tired.
Everyone in this airport seems
tired.

He starts talking and I know some of the words
that are coming out of his mouth,
but my mind feels sticky
and I can't quite catch the meaning.

Back home,
I was always good at English.
I was one of the best in my class
at having pretend conversations.
I think of practicing simple phrases with Fatima
right before I left.
I think of how easy they came to me then—
How are you?
Good. Thank you.
Are you hungry? Would you like to go to lunch?
I would like a sandwich, please.

But this man is not asking me
simple things like
if I am hungry or what I would like to order.
He is asking real questions that
I can barely understand like
Why are you here?
And how long do you plan on staying?

I glance at my mama and her newly swollen stomach
and know this part is my responsibility.
I am the one who knows English.
I am the one who needs to talk,
But I am failing.
Words, all kinds of them, bubble up in my throat
but nothing comes out.

Mama reaches into her purse
and hands the man an envelope.
We watch as the man opens the envelope
and looks through the documents.
He studies each one as though it were a precious
artifact
and every organ in my body holds its breath
as I watch him make up his
mind about us.

Your uncle lives here? he asks me,

giving me
one
more chance to prove myself.
You are coming here to visit him?

Yes, I say.
Yes, yes, yes. It is clear as crystal.
Relief bubbles up inside of me.
One word in English, but it seems to be enough.

The man stamps our paperwork.
Welcome to America.

III.

We are lucky.
  I know this because Mama tells me over
  and over again
  as we walk down the narrow hall
  toward baggage claim.

  Mahzozeen, Mama whispers under her breath.
  And I know she is referring to the fact
  that our papers worked,
  that we are not still stuck in that line,
  that we were not sent back.

  It is so strange to feel lucky
  for something that is making my heart feel so sad.

IV.

My uncle is not what I was expecting.
   He is tailored suits and a fancy wristwatch.
   He is perfect English and a big car that purrs as it
   hums down the street.

   He meets us at the airport with his wife,
   my aunt Michelle,
   and their daughter,
   my cousin, Sarah.

   When he sees my mother,
   his whole face lights up.
   He has my mother's smile.
   He has her eyes,
   my eyes.

   My mother rushes to him,
   and I feel her exhale
   as he wraps his arms around her,
   and something inside me twists.

I don't want my uncle to think that we needed
saving.
I don't want to owe him
anything.

I cross my arms over my chest
to show them—
my uncle, his wife, his daughter—
that I am not a stray animal they need to adopt.

But my resolve
starts to fade when his wife
walks toward me
and clasps my hands
in hers.

Welcome to America, she says.
Her voice sounds like an American movie star—
clear and sprinkled with sugar.

She looks like an American movie star, too.
Honey blond hair,
big light eyes,
casual elegance.

Call me Aunt Michelle.
We're so glad you've come to visit us.

She is looking at me,
telling me
not to worry.
That I don't owe them anything.

I smile at her,
and find my words in English,
Thank you.

V.

My uncle drives us back to his house
    which is in a neighborhood called Clifton.
    Cliff-ton is easier to say than
    Sin-Sa-Nati.

Clifton, I practice saying,
and my cousin Sarah laughs.
She has barely said anything but hello to me,
and now she is laughing.
Laughing at me
and my English pronunciation.

Sarah, Aunt Michelle says,
and I hear the warning in my aunt's voice.
That is something powerful enough to transcend
    oceans:
a mama's ability to say something
without actually saying it.

I don't like this about myself,
but the more I look at my cousin,

my *cool* American cousin,
with her jean shorts that are purposefully ripped,
and sequined T-shirt,
and pale pink lip gloss,
the more I want her to like me.

But from the way
she is staring out the window,
pretending like I don't exist,
I get the feeling that she doesn't care much
whether or not
I like her.

VI.

My uncle's house is so big
    that it could fit four of my old apartments inside of it.
    It has three whole stories
    and shiny wooden floors that
    creak when you step on them.

My uncle Mazin works all the time.
He is an important doctor at an important hospital.
So during the day, it is just
Aunt Michelle
Mama
Sarah
and me.

Our first few days in America are a blur of
mornings that feel like nights
and nights that feel like mornings.
Plates of baked chicken and pasta,
bowls of milky cereal,
and lots and lots of questions from Aunt Michelle.

No matter how tired we are,
Aunt Michelle forces us to get up
and get out.

We take long walks around our new neighborhood.
Aunt Michelle charges ahead,
Mama and me are sandwiched in the middle,
and Sarah walks slowly behind us,
sulking a little.

I keep expecting to see a
cliff in
Clifton
but so far,
I've only found really
big hills,
and even bigger trees.

Clifton is filled with old big houses.
Aunt Michelle tells us that their house
is over one hundred years old and I can tell she is
proud of this, but I'm not sure why.

Everyone back home wants
a new house
not an old one.

When I ask Mama about it,
she says,
Americans don't have much history
so they like things they think are old.

At first, I don't think I will like the
old house with its
creaking
wooden floors
and steep staircases.
Mama and I live up in the bedroom on the
top floor,
the third floor.

But one morning,
when I wake up,
the floor creaks
and it sounds like the house is saying
hello
and that makes me feel less alone.

The old house is
slowly
becoming my friend.
My first American friend.

VII.

When my uncle is home,
    he is always asking
    if we are okay,
    or does Mama need a glass of water?

    I know he means to be nice,
    but it only makes me feel more like a guest
    in his house,
    a visitor,
    a burden.

    Come here, Jude, he says,
    in English.
    Even though I know he speaks Arabic,
    he always speaks to me in English.

    He invites me into his study
    and shows me his speakers
    that can play music
    without any wires.

And his shiny computer
with its big flat screen.

I know he wants me to be impressed,
and I am,
but I try to hide it.

Showing him I'm impressed
feels somehow like a betrayal of Baba,
a betrayal of home.

VIII.

My cousin Sarah is
 chunky platform sandals that
 clomp clomp
 on the hardwood floors of the old house.

She is sparkly pink lip gloss
and nails the color of a sunset on a summer night
and jeans that have shiny sequins on the pockets.

Sometimes she is friendly,
inviting me to sit next to her on the couch
where she watches a television show about
American teenagers who wear fancy clothes and
are trying to figure out
who murdered one of their classmates.

I tell Mama about the show.
Americans are obsessed with murder, she says.
And you made me move here to be safe, I say,
half joking, half not.
Mama shakes her head and tells me to stop watching.

But the very next afternoon,
I sit next to Sarah
on the sun-soaked white leather couch
and watch the American teenagers play detective.

Sarah is less than a year older than me,
but I feel like she is already a
woman
while I am still a little
girl.

She doesn't seem surprised
by all the kissing on the show.
I wonder if she has been kissed herself,
but I'm not brave enough to ask her.

I start to think that Sarah is becoming my friend,
but one night,
I hear her talking with Aunt Michelle.

When will they leave? Sarah says.
My heart sinks as I translate the words
in my head,
the weight of them slowly settling
onto my chest like a stone.

She can't go to my school, Mom, Sarah says.
She doesn't even speak English, she says.

I spend the rest of that night
locked in the bathroom,
whispering to myself in the mirror.
I speak English.

IX.

America is
    full of new things.
    Glittery
    blinking
    in-your-face
    things.

    Everything in America
    moves fast
    and is loud.

    Cars honking
    Traffic lights flashing
    Big billboards advertising
    hamburgers
    drinks
    an entirely new life.

    It seems like everything
    everyone
    is trying to sell you something.

Sometimes I feel dizzy with want,
sometimes I just feel dizzy.

Aunt Michelle takes us shopping
at a mall that feels like it is larger
than my entire town back home.

When I say this to Mama
she scoffs and tells me our town is
not that small
but when she doesn't know I'm looking,
I see her eyes fill with wonder as she takes in
the cold, air-conditioned stores,
each one bigger
fancier
than the last.

In America,
it seems like everyone has money,
new shiny sneakers
bright-colored lipstick
pants that fit just right.

Then I start to notice the man on the corner
with a sign begging people for help,
the tired woman waiting for the bus
with shoes that are cracked at the sole.

America, I realize,
has its sad and tired
parts too.

America,
like every other place in the world,
is a place where some people sleep
and some people
other people
dream.

X.

Sometimes I think I might split in half
    from the ache of missing
    my brother
    Baba
    Fatima
    Auntie Amal
    the ocean
    Chez Mariana
    fruit that tastes like sunshine.

    I even miss the tourists
    and sometimes I even
    miss the smell of fish.

    Sometimes it feels like when I boarded that plane
    to fly to America
    I left my heart behind,
    beating and lonely on the other side of the ocean.

    I talk to Baba through
    my uncle Mazin's fancy computer.

The first time we call him
I sit in my mama's lap while my uncle
presses buttons that make the computer
come alive
and all of a sudden Baba is on the screen.

Both Mama and I squeal with delight.
We tell him about the
old house
and the even
older houses on our street.

We tell him about the big trees
that stretch up high in the sky
and the big hills
and the big cars that we see driving down the street.

Everything is big in America?
he asks, smiling.
Baba is smiling so big
it makes me think
if only for a second
that everything is going to be okay,
that someday soon we'll all be
together
again.
Mama asks him about the store

and he says everything is good
but his smile fades.
Until now, I never knew you could see
fear
through a computer screen.

Baba says our town is safe
but there are still protests
and there are still tanks in nearby towns.

When he talks about the protests
and the tanks in the nearby towns,
we all tense and
my heart is thinking
Where is Issa?
Do you see him?
Do you miss him?
But my mouth is silent,
my lips shut like a
closed door.

When Baba ends the call
and it's just Mama and me left in Uncle Mazin's study,
I ask Mama about Issa.

Her big eyes go sad,
she kisses my face,

85

and tells me not to worry,
but it's hard to do that when I can see,
and smell,
the worry all over her.

XI.

Aunt Michelle wears her hair in a long loose braid
and has a band of bracelets that jangle on her wrist
when she walks.

She shows me how to use the dishwasher,
an appliance we did not have back home,
and how to use the microwave,
thirty seconds to defrost a piece of frozen bread,
approximately two minutes to reheat a dinner plate.

I love the way Aunt Michelle
greets me every morning with a plate of pancakes.
The way she speaks slowly
so that I can understand her,
and always smiles like she understands me,
even when I know my accent is thick
and I have put the words in the wrong order.

I love how she shows me all the flowers in her garden,
pointing each one out and saying its English name

slowly.
Rose,
tulip,
marigold.

Mama is not sure about Aunt Michelle.
But I already feel comfortable
gliding around barefoot in her kitchen,
singing along with her
to an old Whitney Houston song.
She tells me that I can always
put on any song that I want
all I have to do is ask.

Aunt Michelle's old house is washed with sun.
She leaves all the windows open.
And it is decorated with white pillows,
white chairs, and white couches.

Too much white, Mama says.
Boring, Mama says.

Once I hear Mama ask Uncle Mazin,
I don't see anything from home here.
Uncle Mazin turns to her and says,
This is home.

XII.

Aunt Michelle loves anything
    French.
She studied French literature at university
where she met my uncle.

He says he fell in love with her the moment
he saw her.
Aunt Michelle shakes her head when he says this,
but her face turns red and she looks so
happy that I know she
believes him.

Mama also shakes her head
at this story.
Aunt Michelle pretends not to notice,
but I know she does.

Mama says,
She's too American.
I say,

She is American.
Mama says,
She doesn't speak a word of Arabic.
I say,
Why would she? She's American.
She says,
She has made Mazin forget his home.
I want to say,
This is his home now,
but I look at Mama's belly
and don't say anything.

XIII.

Aunt Michelle takes Sarah and me out to lunch
    at a French restaurant.
    We eat sandwiches on baguette bread—

    Aunt Michelle and Sarah get their sandwiches
    with ham
    and I want to,
    but then I think of Mama,
    all alone in my uncle's house,
    and what she would think if she saw me eating ham,
    and I order just cheese and tomato.

    Back home,
    food was
    rice
    lamb
    fish
    hummus
    pita bread
    olives

feta cheese
za'atar with olive oil.

Here,
that food is
Middle Eastern food.
Baguettes are French food.
Spaghetti is Italian food.
Pizza is both American and Italian,
depending on which restaurant you go to.

Every food has a label.
It is sorted and assigned.

Just like I am no longer
a girl.
I am a Middle Eastern girl.
A Syrian girl.
A Muslim girl.

Americans love labels.
They help them know what to expect.
Sometimes, though,
I think labels stop them from
thinking.

What do you think? Aunt Michelle asks
when the dessert comes.

It is a chocolate tart.
It is delicious.
I look around the restaurant,
at the stiff white linen tablecloths,
at the framed pictures of the Eiffel Tower,
at the servers wearing pin-striped pants.

It's very French, I say.
I wonder if the words that come out of my mouth
make any sense
at all.

Aunt Michelle and Sarah smile
and that's when I know—
I am finally speaking a language
that they
understand.

XIV.

The night before
  the first day of school,
  a storm breaks across
  the sky.

  I watch the lightning
  streak
  and the thunder
  boom
  from the window on the third floor.

  I press my face up against the glass
  and say, *American storms are so strong.*
  The wind bends the tree,
  and there is a hiccup of fear in my chest,
  but the trees stay strong.

  We have storms back home, Mama says.
  She is lying in bed, her hands propped on her belly,
  which is growing larger every day.

Mama always does this.
If I say I like something,
if I'm impressed with something,
in America,
she reminds me that we have the same thing back
in Syria.

I usually ignore her, but tonight,
it is like the storm is inside of me too
and I am tired of being quiet.

Don't you want me to like it here?
I am tired of being the tree in the wind
that is always pushed,
but never allowed to fall down.

Of course, she says.
I walk over to the bed
and hoist myself up onto the mattress.
Mama wraps her arms around me,
pulling me close to her,
and she smells like she always has,
agarwood oil and rosewater.
It is the smell of home,
of love,
of safety.
It is a smell that makes me feel like it is okay
for me to say anything.

Why did you bring me here? I ask, the same question
I am always asking,
but am never getting a satisfactory answer to.

You know why, habibti, Mama says,
and she sounds so tired,
and I almost decide to drop it,
but then the thunder booms
and I feel it in my chest and I say,
It's like you want me to hate it here.

Of course I don't.

But you always tell me things are better at home.

I am scared you will forget.

If you didn't want me to forget, we shouldn't have left.

Mama takes my face in her hands,
she pulls me centimeters from her,
and it feels like we are sharing one
breath.

*Don't you see? I know you will have a better life here,
but that breaks my heart.
You are too young to understand, Jude,
but someday you will.*

Lightning cracks across the sky
and I lean against her
and she accepts my weight,
pulling me into her arms.

PART THREE
Staying

I.

My new school is three blocks
    from my new house.

Sarah and I are supposed to walk together
but on the morning of the first day,
the sky is pouring rain
so Aunt Michelle drops us both off at the front steps.

Sarah bounds in
and leaves me staring up
at the enormous old building
which is new to me.

Other students rush by me,
but I stay planted at the foot of the steps,
the rain dripping on my head.

I am less afraid of getting wet
than I am of what is inside.
I swallow the knot in my throat

and replay my brother's parting words to me,
Be brave.

Be brave, be brave, be brave
echoes like a chorus in my head as I climb the stairs
and enter my brand-new world.

II.

I am given a schedule by a nice lady in the front office.
    She asks if I will be able to read it
    and if I need help,
    and the answers to her two questions are
    probably not
    and *probably yes,*
    yet somehow I reverse them and I end up wandering
    down the long halls,
    taking wrong turn after wrong turn,
    eventually ending up in the right place,
    but still somehow feeling like it
    is the wrong one.

    I have seven different classes,
    English,
    science,
    social studies,
    math,
    art,
    gym,
    and ESL.

ESL means
English as a second language.
It is a class for kids like me,
kids whose English is sticky and slow.
Kids who were from somewhere else,
but are here now.

My first class of the day is math.
I arrive late.
I know I am late because I hear the bell ring while
I am still wandering around in the empty hall,
peering into every classroom,
willing it to be room 202,
Pre-Algebra with Mr. Anderson.

Pre is an English preposition that
means before.
Pre Jude knew the way to all her classes,
Pre Jude never showed up late.

When I finally find the classroom,
everyone else is already sitting at their desks.
Mr. Anderson greets me with a patient smile
and motions toward an empty desk
in the second row
on the left side.

I walk across the classroom
and I feel everyone's eyes on me.
Pre Jude reveled in her classmates' attention,
but now I just want to blend in.

III.

Mr. Anderson passes out a packet of papers
    that explain what we will be studying this year.
    He goes over the rules of his class,
    his expectations,
    how much homework he will assign.

    The whole class groans at the mention of
    homework.
    It is a communal moment I do not participate in
    because once I've figured out what
    Mr. Anderson means by "homework,"
    he's already talking about something else.

    Now that I've gotten that
    housekeeping out of the way,
    let's do some practice problems
    and see what you guys already know.

    As he grabs a piece of chalk
    and writes problems on the board,

I think about the word
housekeeping:
the upkeep of the home,
the management of household affairs.

Does Mr. Anderson mean that
our classroom is like a house?
His house?
Our house?

I look at the practice problems on the board.
I know the answer to two of the three.
I like thinking in numbers.
Numbers are easier than letters.
They have not changed on me.

He asks for volunteers.
I almost raise my hand,
but then realize I would have to explain my answer
not only in numbers
but in words,
letters.

I do not raise my hand.
The whole classroom is silent,
still,
and then a boy seated in the front row volunteers.

He walks to the front of the classroom.
He is wearing a T-shirt
with a photograph of a galaxy on it,
millions and millions of twinkling stars.

The boy works quickly
and when he is done,
he walks back to his desk without saying anything.

Mr. Anderson checks his work,
and claps as he announces that all
of the boy's answers
are correct.

I stare
at the back of the boy's head,
imagining and thinking about all
those swirling stars on the front of his shirt,
all those different worlds.

IV.

When I get to Mrs. Ravenswood's ESL class,
my fourth class of the day,
I almost don't go inside.

At first, I am embarrassed to be in
Mrs. Ravenswood's ESL class.

I think of what Sarah said to Aunt Michelle.
I speak English
thunders in my brain.

Mrs. Ravenswood is younger
than any teacher I have ever had.
She wears a skirt with red polka dots on it
and has a smile like a cup of milky warm tea;
it welcomes and comforts you all at the same time.

I am one of four kids in the class.
There is me,
Grace, who is from Korea

Ben, who is from China
and Omar, who is from Somalia.

We all sit together
in the center of the classroom
at a round wooden table.

Mrs. Ravenswood has us go around
the table and introduce ourselves.
She says,
Tell me something you like
and tell me something you find confusing about English.

Grace starts.
She says she likes that in English,
in America,
she is called Grace.
She has a different name at home,
but her parents let her choose
a new English name when they moved to America.
She says that she likes that Grace feels like
a whole
new
exciting
identity.

She says she doesn't like

that lots of words in English
sound the same
like *knight* and *night*
and *weather* and *whether*
and sometimes it's hard for her to figure out
which is which.

Ben
Omar
and me all laugh a little when Grace says this,
each of us looking at one another,
a little afraid to admit
that we relate to what Grace said,
but so relieved that there is someone else
in this school
in this city
in this country
who feels the same way
about *knight* and *night*.

Ben shares that he likes
American slang words like
cool and *awesome*
and especially the word *dough*,
which he explains he recently learned
means money.

Dough, he says,
and then Omar says, *Yeah, that's a COOL word,*
and we all laugh again.

I was wrong about not
wanting to be in Mrs. Ravenswood's room.

V.

My school is filled with kids who do not look like me.
    Kids with pale freckled skin,
    kids with hair the color of summertime corn.
    And kids with skin darker than mine,
    kids shorter than me,
    and kids taller than me.

    I have never seen so many
    different types of people in one place.

    I write to Fatima
    and tell her
    that sometimes it feels like
    the whole world
    lives at my new school.

VI.

Sarah and I don't have any of the same classes,
    but during the second week of school,
    I see her in the hallway.

I raise my hand to wave,
my face breaking into a smile,
but she turns away from me,
like I'm invisible.

She is leaning against a locker,
surrounded by her group of friends.
All her friends are pretty
with shiny hair
and clothes that look like they cost
a lot of *dough*.

They stand in a circle
that does not open for me.

At home that night,

Sarah pretends like nothing happened.
Why didn't you say hi to me today? I ask.
Sarah takes a bite of her bagel,
which Aunt Michelle has smeared
with cream cheese and jelly.

Her eyes look away from me,
focused on the TV.
We are watching another show
about glamorous American teenagers.

Sorry, she finally says,
after a very long pause.
I was just busy with my friends.

I want to say,
Aren't I your friend?
Don't you want me to meet
your other friends?

But I don't.
I take a bite of my bagel
and almost spit it out with surprise
when Sarah says,
Will you teach me some Arabic words?

You're so lucky, she says.

I wish I spoke Arabic.
At first, I don't understand why she is saying this,
but then I see the way she looks longingly at
Uncle Mazin and Mama who are
in the kitchen
speaking in Arabic
and laughing.

Lucky, I whisper to myself that night.
I wonder if I say it enough times,
if it will start to feel true,
come true.

There is an Arabic proverb that says:
Her luck splits open rocks.
I am still waiting to feel like the force
and less like the rocks.

VII.

Sarah is never by herself at school.
    Whenever I see her,
    she is surrounded by friends
    who follow her around like
    the sea hugs the shore,
    drifting in and out,
    but always coming back.

    We have the same lunch break,
    but she never invites me to sit at her table,
    which is in the back of the cafeteria,
    by the windows.

    I tell myself that she doesn't invite me
    because there isn't any space,
    but then one day,
    I notice there is an empty seat
    at the very end of the table.

    I hold my breath when I see Sarah
    walking in my direction.

She is trailed by a girl
wearing a sparkly headband
and another girl with leather boots
that I try to memorize
so I can describe them to Fatima
in a letter later because I think
she would love them.

My whole body rings
with anticipation as I wait
for Sarah's invitation.

But it doesn't come.

She and her friends walk
right past me
up to the counter where
they each purchase a cookie.

Wednesdays are the best,
I hear Sarah say
as she walks back to her table,
triumphantly holding her cookie.

I get up from the table
where I have been sitting
by myself

and run to the bathroom,
where I hide in a stall,
and sob
and wonder if this lonely ache
inside of me
will ever go away.

VIII.

Ben is telling me about his old apartment back in China.
  I used to live in the clouds, he says,
  in a very tall building
  that looked out over all of Shanghai.
  I have never been to Ben's old house
  or even to China,
  but I can imagine it because of Ben's
  excellent English.

  Ben was in Mrs. Ravenswood's class last year
  and I wonder if he's done this exercise before.
  I tell myself this to feel better
  about the fact I have absolutely no idea
  what to say to describe my old home.

  I can see it—
  the tiny kitchen that was always filled with sunlight,
  the flat roof of our apartment building that was
  dotted with TV satellites,
  but my mind doesn't find the words in English
  to say what I want to say.

It's okay, Ben says,
giving me a warm smile.
I think this exercise is really hard, too.

We switch partners and Omar
tells me about how hot the sun was
and how he always woke up to
the sound of his mother singing
in the kitchen.

Grace tells me that at her old home
she used to have to climb steps up to her bed.
But here in America, she says,
My bed is on the ground.
She blinks and then says, *Floor?*
Is floor better?

Do you like it better? I ask.
She gives me a little smile,
not saying yes or no, only
It's different.

Class is almost over,
and Mrs. Ravenswood says she has a surprise for us.
We all look at each other excitedly,
thinking that she is going to let us watch
a snippet of an American movie—
a treat she sometimes allows us

when we've worked hard in class.

But instead she brings out a box
of cupcakes.
She holds one up to show us
how it is decorated.
Like soccer balls! she says.
To celebrate Omar.

We learn that Omar
has made the soccer team.
We all clap for him.
His accomplishment,
somehow,
almost,
feels like our own.

I still don't understand the word
soccer, Omar says as he devours his cupcake,
icing smeared at the side of his mouth.
Feet.
He points to his feet.
You play with your feet.
Football.

This makes all of us laugh.

IX.

One night, Uncle Mazin asks me
    if he can take me out to dinner.
    At first, I think Mama,
    Aunt Michelle,
    and Sarah will be invited too.

    But soon it is just me and him
    gliding down the street
    in the leather seats
    of his fancy car
    that rides so smoothly down the road
    that you forget you are even in a car.

    We go to a restaurant with dim lighting
    with servers who have very serious expressions
    who bring out plates with baked potatoes
    and large pieces of meat.

    In America,
    we call this a steak,

Uncle Mazin says,
gesturing from his plate
to mine.

I can tell he
wants me to be impressed
by the hunk of meat
sitting untouched on the plate.

I cut into it
and let out a cry.
It's bleeding, I shriek.

Uncle Mazin laughs
and shakes his head.
No, he says.
It's perfect.
In Syria, they overcook meat.

I look at the light pink
of the meat,
my stomach turning at his words,
at the small puddle of blood
on my plate.

I pick at the baked potato instead.
I have been learning that in America,

they add something called butter
to everything.

I may not be able
to see the appeal of bleeding meat,
but butter,
I understand.

Are you happy here? Uncle Mazin
asks me as he finishes his
bleeding steak.
I can hear the worry in his voice,
how much he wants me to say yes.

I don't answer him.
Instead I say,
What is an entrée?
It sounds like the word
enter, but it isn't the beginning of
the meal because that word is—
I pause and try to pronounce
App-e-tizer.

He smiles,
but not in a way that makes
me think he finds me childish
or uneducated.

He smiles at me
like he is seeing an old picture
of himself
or reliving a memory
that he had almost forgotten.

It gets easier, he says.
Give it time.

And that's when I realize
my uncle hasn't been showing me
all his fancy stuff to impress me,
but to convince me.

To convince himself.

X.

I am rounding the corner
    to go up the next flight of stairs
    when I hear Sarah call out to me.

    Come here, she says,
    inviting me into her room,
    where I have never been before.

    It is the biggest bedroom
    I have ever seen,
    a giant bed with a white lace canopy
    is pressed against the back wall
    and there is a white desk
    perfectly organized with all
    different colored pens
    and paper clips.

    It seems like the kind
    of place where dreams
    could grow and
    live.

I can't believe Dad took
you to Jeff Ruby's.

Sarah says *you*
like she is accusing me
of a crime.

Do you know the last time
he took me out to dinner,
just me and him?
she asks, and I don't
say anything because I don't
know the answer.

Yeah, she says softly
and looks out the big window
of her room
at the moon that is newly swollen
hanging so low in the sky
that it almost tricks you
into thinking you could touch it.
Me either.

I stand there for
a couple more moments.
I can tell she wants me to leave,
but I want her to ask me to.

I am tired of all these
guessing games.

I need to finish
my history homework,
she finally says.
Her voice isn't mean,
only sad.

As I leave her room
I think of the Arabic proverb that says:
She cannot give what she does not have.

I have never really understood
what that means,
but it seems wise
and like I might be learning
to better understand it now.

XI.

Mama cannot believe that
    Uncle Mazin doesn't go to mosque.
    He makes excuses like he is busy with
    work
    family
    life,
    but Mama won't hear any of it.

    She finds a mosque on Clifton Avenue.
    It's only a ten-minute walk, she says to me,
    proud that she has found it,
    proud that she is attending,
    proud that she is walking there on her own.

    Sometimes when I am at school,
    she goes to the mosque and takes an English class.
    She has found her own version
    of Mrs. Ravenswood's class.
    When I get home from school,
    I practice with her.

Hello?
How are you?
Good. Thank you.
Where is the bathroom?
My name is Sahar. What is your name?

One day, she says to me,
in English,
I miss home.

I hug her tight,
so proud of her.

Me too, I say.
Me too.

XII.

A few weeks later,
    Mama takes a nap in the late afternoon
    because the new baby is eating all of her energy.
    You're going to be a troublemaker, she says,
    and even though she is speaking to her belly,
    speaking to the baby,
    I can tell she is thinking about Issa.

    Aunt Michelle is busy raking leaves
    out of the backyard,
    Sarah is over at a friend's house,
    and Uncle Mazin is where he always is, work.

    That means that I am free
    to walk around our neighborhood.
    Mama doesn't like for me to walk alone
    because she worries I might get lost.
    Aunt Michelle tells her I will be fine,
    as long as it is light out.

The sun is still out
even though the days are getting darker and darker
earlier and earlier.

I walk down the sidewalks
that are old and cracked,
past wooden houses with slanted roofs,
painted beautiful pastel colors.

I wave at a man getting off the bus,
a boy on a skateboard,
a woman with two large grocery bags.
They smile,
and I smile.

I make it to Ludlow Avenue,
which is lined with shops and restaurants
that smell like burnt vanilla and curry and
fried eggs.

I have written
five letters
to Fatima to tell her about my new neighborhood
new city
new country
new life.

In each of those letters,
I've told her about Ludlow Avenue.
It is not
b i g g e r
than any of the main streets back home,
but it is so different.
Different because of the different
shops
restaurants
and people.

It is a tiny street,
but it feels like the whole world
is living there.

XIII.

It is on Ludlow Avenue that I discover
   a Middle Eastern restaurant,
   which back home would just be called
   simply
   a restaurant.

   The Middle Eastern restaurant I discover
   is called Ali Baba.
   It is squeezed between a shop called
   Pangea—
   which does not seem to sell prehistoric supercontinents,
   but ladies' hats and scarves—
   and a restaurant called
   The Great Wall,
   which sells food that my cousin Sarah tells me is
   Chinese.

   The first few times,
   I only walk by Ali Baba.
   I do not go inside.

I am scared that I do not belong in
a Middle Eastern restaurant
in the middle of America.

I am scared that the only place
in Middle America that I belong
is a Middle Eastern restaurant.

On the seventh walk-by,
I decide to swallow my fear.
I pretend I am my brother Issa,
deciding to march in the streets,

deciding to never call his sister.

I am bold
and fearless
and do not care what people think.

I push open the door,
and at once, I feel at home,
greeted by old friends
the smell of cumin and thyme,
the strong scent of Arabic coffee brewing on a stove
in the back of the kitchen.

Marhaba, I call out,
more to the smells than to

anyone,
but a girl emerges from the kitchen.

I recognize her.
I have seen her in the halls.
She is the only girl in my school
who wears a headscarf.

She is taller than me,
but has a young face.
Her head is wrapped with a scarf the color of
an eggplant
or a bruise.

She asks in Arabic,
if I speak Arabic,
and even though her Arabic is good,
I can tell she is a native English speaker,
by the shape of her mouth,
and the way the words slide out
unbent by the athletic tongue of someone
who was born speaking Arabic.

She motions for me to take a seat
at a table in the back of the restaurant.
Wait for me, she says,
this time in English.
I drum on the table with my fingers,

in the same way I used to watch Issa do,
when he would take me out to the sandwich shop,
and we would wait for our order of falafel and hummus
and extra tahini sauce.

It feels like it has been a very long time,
too much waiting.
(I am always saying *too* in English
when I mean *so*.)
And I am about to leave,
but then the girl comes back.
She has a tray full of
shawarma
falafel
hummus
pickles
olives
fresh bread.

My mouth waters
and then I see at the end of the tray,
there is a small metal teapot
and it looks exactly like the one Auntie Amal used to
pour us our tea during *asroneyeh*.

My eyes water and tears spill out
and I think the girl is going to ask me
what

is wrong
but instead she says,
I'm Layla.
And I say,
I'm Jude.

XIV.

These are the things I know about Layla:
    She is in grade eight,
    whereas I am in grade seven.

I also know that her baba,
Samir, is from Lebanon,
and her mama,
Dasia, is also from there.
They run the restaurant,
Ali Baba,
together.

Her mama manages the kitchen,
and her baba manages
everything else
which is an American phrase
that I don't quite understand.

Layla has never been to Lebanon
and she picks my brain for every

tiny
detail
about the Middle East.

You're so lucky you've been there, she says.
I'm here now, I say.
But that's lucky too, she insists.
And I know she is thinking of those towns
nearby mine,
the ones that have been overtaken
by the men with the stolen tanks.
The ones where people are afraid
to walk down the street.

Lucky, I repeat.

XV.

One of my favorite things
    about my new neighborhood is that
    the university is right nearby
    so in the afternoons, there are always students walking
    up
    and down
    the sidewalks, holding coffee, and talking fast.

I like to sometimes pretend that Issa is one of them,
carrying his backpack on only one shoulder,
and talking fast on his way back
to his basement apartment.

I spend a lot of time walking around outside,
my hands tucked into the pockets of the fancy new coat
that Aunt Michelle
bought for me.

The coat is the color of roses
and lined with white fleece.

It is as beautiful as it is soft.
So beautiful in fact that when I showed it to Mama
I expected her to scoff,
because it came from Aunt Michelle,
but even Mama couldn't deny that it is
beautiful.

And I feel beautiful when I wear it.
Beautiful and
American,
gliding down Ludlow Avenue,
past the students talking fast,
past the shop that sells ladies' hats,
all the way to visit Layla at her parents' restaurant
where I am sometimes put to work.
I help scrape old food into the trash bins,
but am always in return
fed falafel and extra pieces of baklava that come on big
trays from a bakery in Detroit.

Layla and I compare notes about school.
I don't see her that often in the halls
because she is not in my grade,
and she doesn't have to be in Mrs. Ravenswood's class
because her mind does not get stuck
on simple words like *put*
and *on*

and *too*
and *so*
and when to use which one.

I tell Layla how much I am liking school,
but that I don't have any very close friends yet,
no one like Fatima,
and then her face falls and she says,
But you have me.

I nod because I know Layla wants to be like my Fatima
and she is my good friend,
but no one is
like Fatima.
I promised Fatima that I wouldn't forget her,
and I break a lot of things,
but I try not to break promises.

So I go on telling Layla about
the other people that I have met:
Lauren, a girl in my science class with wavy hair
who lets me borrow a pencil when I forget mine,
and Grace from Mrs. Ravenswood's class,
who helps me practice converting measurements into
    inches.

I think about mentioning

the boy from my math class who always wears
T-shirts with pictures of space,
but I haven't exactly met him yet.
I've only stared at the back of his head.

Wow, Layla says.
She sounds like such an American when she says wow.
You really do like it here.

I shrug,
and she gives me a look,
which I don't quite understand.

It is part surprise,
and part waiting.
It is all unknown.

XVI.

One night it is rainy
    when I walk home from the restaurant.
    I wrap my beautiful coat around my shoulders,
    and the rain that feels almost like ice hits my nose.

    My beautiful coat is
    not enough to keep me from the chill,
    and two days later,
    I find myself stuck in bed,
    feeling so cold
    and shaky,
    the chill from that night is trapped inside my bones,
    even though the temperature says I am burning up.

    Mama takes care of me,
    sitting at the end of my bed,
    singing songs in Arabic,
    brushing hair away from my sweaty forehead
    so she can kiss me.

I am drowsy with sickness
and in the first few moments after my eyes flutter open
and I hear my mama singing,
I think we're at home.
My whole heart pulses
with happiness.
I hold my breath,
waiting to see Baba,
Issa.

But then I hear the wood floors creak
as Aunt Michelle comes in and out
with medicine that tastes like sour berries
and soups made of salty broths,
and I know I am not back home,
but here,
in this home.

I look outside my window
at the leaves from the big trees that are
falling
to the ground,
at the cold rain that is
falling
to the ground,
and yet,
something inside of me is no longer

falling.

It is
rising.

XVII.

Most times at dinner,
    it is always
    Mama
    me
    Sarah
    and Aunt Michelle.

Sometimes my uncle Mazin joins us
on days when he does not have to work late,
and those are the best days because
we all love
Uncle Mazin.

When Uncle Mazin is there,
even Mama smiles and eats almost
every bite of food off her plate,
every bite of the meal that Aunt Michelle made,
the meals Mama thinks are
too
strange.

Aunt Michelle tells me
that she gets most of her recipes online.
She shows me website after website
that is filled with delicious photographs of food
and also photographs of women dressed in beautiful
outfits sprawled across beautiful furniture
in their beautiful houses.

Aunt Michelle lets me click through
the recipes on her iPad,
and sometimes even lets me choose
which ones we should try.
My mouth waters at the images of
pumpkin risotto
black bean tostadas
tofu tacos.
These are words that I don't quite know
what they mean,
but my eyes translate for my stomach.

One night, though, Mama wins and Aunt Michelle
lets her cook dinner.
Mama does not find her recipe online.
She finds it in her memory,
her heart.

I watch her as she fries up the cauliflower in lots of oil
and roasts the lamb with even more oil

and on the table there are loaves and loaves
of pita bread
that she got fresh from Layla's mom and toasted up
right on the stove,
right over the open flame,
just like how she used to do back home.

I can tell Sarah is a little unsure about the food,
but soon she is piling the crispy cauliflower
into her mouth
and smiling and telling Aunt Michelle
all about her day,
much more talkative than she usually is.

Uncle Mazin is smiling too,
and he looks at Mama and says,
This tastes like home.

XVIII.

When Layla first tells me about the school musical,
    I don't understand what she is saying.
    My school back home did not put on plays.
    School was for
    serious subjects like science
    and math,
    things that can be measured
    and calculated.

It's a big deal, Layla says.
This is one of Layla's favorite phrases.
I've saved it for the next time I talk to Issa,
I think he will find it
funny.

So many people try out, Layla says.
And people from all over the city come to watch on opening night.
Last year, it was written about in the paper.

Are you going to try out? I ask

and Layla gives me the same look
that she gave me before—
the one that is part surprise
part waiting
part unknown.

No, she finally says.
Laughing in the way
that has nothing to do with humor.
I'm going to work on the sets.
You should do it, too.
It's fun.

I don't say yes but I go
with her to the meeting that takes place after school
in our school's big theater.
The theater is beautiful with a wide wooden stage
and velvet plush seats that you sink into
when you sit down.
The seats remind me of the movie theater
that Sammy took Fatima and me to
that one summer.

I cannot believe this school
my school
has an auditorium like this.
As I watch the teacher,

Mrs. Bloom,
talk about the spring musical up on the stage,
the lights beaming right onto her face,
I try to imagine what it would be like to stand up there.

I can't imagine it.
I can't stop imagining it.

I look from
side
to side
and see so many faces that are also imagining it.

One of them I recognize.
It is Sarah.
She is sitting with three of her friends a few rows in
    front of Layla and me.

Layla nudges my shoulder as if to ask,
Do you see her?
I nod.
I wonder if Sarah is thinking
about trying out for the play
or if she wants to make sets like Layla.

Everyone gets very quiet while Mrs. Bloom talks about
    the guidelines for the tryout:

a two-minute monologue
and a song.
The tryouts will take place the week
we get back from winter break.

Mrs. Bloom paces the stage,
the heels of her boots echoing against the wood,
and I imagine it again:

Me, walking on that stage.
My footsteps echoing.
My voice radiating through the room.
All the eyes in the entire room focused on
me.

At the end of the meeting,
Mrs. Bloom sets down some packets on
the stage.
I follow Layla,
fully intending to take the one
about joining the stage and tech crew.

But at the last minute,
I grab a tryout packet too.

XIX.

Math class is tough for me
        because I usually know how to solve
        for *x* or *y*
        but I don't know how to
        explain how I know.

        So I stay quiet
        while Mr. Anderson calls
        on other students to answer
        the sample problems
        like the boy who almost always
        wears a space T-shirt.

        I stare at his back,
        at all of those stars.
        Sometimes it is comforting
        to me to remember how vast
        the universe is.
        How small our galaxy is in comparison.
        How I still live in the

same galaxy as
Baba
and Issa and Fatima and Auntie Amal.

I glance out the window
at the trees that are
shedding their final leaves.

I wonder if it is exhausting
to be a tree.
To lose something,
year after year,
only to trust that it will
someday grow back.

XX.

Winter arrives with a thud
    two weeks before Thanksgiving.
    Our teachers tell us that winter doesn't officially start
    until December 21st,
    but the snow outside tells a different story.

    At school,
    we all wear sweaters,
    turtlenecks—an American word for a clothing item
        that makes me laugh—
    hats,
    gloves.
    One day, the heater in the building of our school gives
        out,
    and we all keep our coats on inside.
    It feels like an
    adventure we are all having
    together.

During Mrs. Ravenswood's class, Omar shivers.
It is never this cold in Somalia.
He is surprised that I am not bothered by the cold.
Syria, I say, *is a country with many climates.*
Everyone in the class seems surprised by this.
I like being able to surprise people.

In Mrs. Ravenswood's class, we practice
talking about the weather.
At first I feel silly,
practicing with Grace—
It is cold, you will need a sweater.
Is it windy?
The sky is cloudy.

But then I start to like being able
to put into words
the thoughts that are in my head.

Grace feels the same way, she tells me.
But do you worry that you're going to forget your mother tongue?
It makes me smile the way Grace calls Korean
her mother tongue.
That means Arabic is my mother tongue,
And it is my mama's tongue,
but I've never thought of it that way before.

No, I say
because I've also never thought I would forget it.

What word would you miss the most? she asks.
I laugh and shake my head.
I'm not going to forget
a
single
word.

And then Grace gives me that look
that I've seen before on Layla's face,
on Sarah's face,
even once on Fatima's face—
like they are waiting for me to understand something
they have already learned.

I don't think you have to forget
in order to learn, I say,
making sure my English is perfect.
Grace smiles at this,
and I think she's as proud as I am
that my English is getting better every day.

XXI.

Bad news doesn't happen in real life
    the way that it does in movies.

    In movies, you are warned.
    The music gets scary,
    the sky goes dark,
    and you can see the shadows coming in.

    But on the day Mama tells me that Issa is gone,
    the sky is bright,
    and I'm happy because in math class
    my teacher, Mr. Anderson, asked me a question
    in front of everyone and I got the answer right.
    In English.
    In front of everyone.

    So when I burst through the front door
    of Uncle Mazin and Aunt Michelle's house—
    which I am beginning to think of as my house too—
    I am not expecting to find Mama waiting for me

in the chair by the big bay window,
her face illuminated by the watery winter light.

She stands up from the chair
and hugs me tight,
so tight that
I swear I feel the baby inside of her,
kicking against her stomach.

No scary music,
no thunderstorm,
this is my warning:
what is coming next is going to hurt.

She tells me Issa has left home—
and when I try to interrupt her
to say that I already know that—
She interrupts me right back,
her eyes flashing,
stunning me into silence.

She tells me that Issa has left
to go to another town
one of those towns
taken over by men
who are fighting with the government
and who are also fighting with people like Issa

ordinary people
who only want to see Syria grow up
into a better version of itself.

Where? I ask.
I want specifics.
I need to be able to imagine him.
There is a panic
climbing up my spine,
crawling into my chest.
I feel like screaming,
but I can't
even open my mouth.

Near Aleppo. Mama's voice is barely a whisper
but her words
thunder
in my ears.
Aleppo.

Even a girl like me,
a girl who likes movies more than news,
a girl who didn't pay
much attention to what was happening,
knows Aleppo is synonymous with war.
And death.

Mama hugs me
and I hold her back.
Sometimes all you can do is
hold on.

XXII.

I wake up early,
　　tiptoeing out of bed before Mama rouses from sleep.
　　We still sleep on the same queen-size mattress.
　　Aunt Michelle is always offering
　　to get another bed for me,
　　to rearrange the room,
　　to make it more comfortable for us.

　　I used to think that at any moment
　　I was going to feel ready to sleep in my own
　　American
　　bed.

　　But ever since I heard the news about Issa,
　　I can't imagine not having the security of Mama's
　　solid body there in the middle of the night
　　when my sleep breaks
　　and I am filled with a terror of not quite knowing
　　where I am or
　　where I am going.

I wrap my arms around her
and I hold on,
I hold on to that feeling of home.

But in the early mornings,
I summon my courage to leave the sleepy security
of our shared bed
and climb down the stairs to the kitchen
where Aunt Michelle is always already awake,
nursing a big mug of coffee
staring out the window into the backyard
where the trees have
recently shed their limbs
and in a certain light,
the branches look like snakes wriggling against the sky.

Someday,
I am going to be brave enough to ask Aunt Michelle
what she is looking for.

Until then,
I am working on being brave in smaller steps,
opening my eyes and seeing and learning.
Aunt Michelle has started leaving
Uncle Mazin's newspaper
out for me to read,
and I comb through the articles that I know he has
    already read before me

because his sticky jam fingerprints mark the pages.

There is something comforting
about the fact my uncle has read the articles
first.
Even if he doesn't talk
out loud
about what is happening in Syria.

Like my uncle,
I am hungry to read every word I can about
Aleppo
about the families from my country
who were not as lucky as me,
who are fleeing from towns that are under siege
taken over by violent radicals
or by the government under the guise of stopping
violent radicals.

I read about how Europe and
America
no longer want to allow people who come from my
country
to move to their shores for safety.

I read about families stranded on shaky boats,
trapped in refugee camps.

I search every day for a mention of my brother
and I never find one.
I search every day for a clue about why I deserve
to be here in Aunt Michelle's kitchen,
safe
and fed.
When so many others
just like me are not.

Lucky. I am learning how to say it
over and over again in English.
I am learning how it tastes—
sweet with promise
and bitter with responsibility.

XXIII.

The day before Thanksgiving
in every one of my classes,
we are asked to talk about what we are grateful for.

Mrs. Ravenswood explains
that Thanksgiving is a time
when Americans
give thanks.
T-h-a-n-k-s.
She breaks down the word for us
into tiny pieces so we can digest it,
think about it.

Ben shares that he is thankful his father
will have a long break
from work soon and his whole family
is taking a trip to New York City.

Grace smiles at Mrs. Ravenswood
and says she is thankful

her English is getting better,
and we all applaud her.

Omar goes next.
It takes him a moment to speak,
and I wonder if like me,
he is searching for something to say.
If he is struggling with how you can feel so lucky
and unlucky
at the very same time.

I am grateful to be here, he says quietly.
We all nod,
because we all know what Omar is trying to say.
What he can't quite manage to say in English,
what is almost impossible to say—

we are lucky to be here
when so many others aren't.
But we don't understand the luck of
why or how
just the luck.

The better our English gets,
the better we get at reading the newspaper articles,
the signs,
hearing the radio,

about how so many people don't want us here.
Finally, it is my turn.
I want to say,
I don't feel lucky or grateful because my brother has gone to a
war zone
and I don't know
if he will ever return.

But instead I say,
I am grateful for my brother.
I talk about him.
I talk more than I am supposed to,
but they don't seem to mind.

At first, I think I want to tell them
about how brave Issa is
how he is risking his life because
he believes so much in a better version
of his country.
But then I think about why I love my brother and
I do love that he is brave,
but I also love the way his whole body shakes
when he laughs
and how he can hit all the notes when he sings
Whitney Houston
and how when I was younger,
he would put me on his shoulders

when we were walking down by the sea and
I felt like the woman
from the Arabic myth
who can see so far into the distance
that she can see the future.

Mrs. Ravenswood helps me with the English words
that I stumble on
and nothing comes out the exact way I want it to.
My voice cracks more than once—
from sadness,
from frustration that I can't say
what I truly want to say.

I do not have the right words
to describe the space between
my brother's eyebrows
that wrinkles when he is laughing
or deep in thought.

But in talking about him,
in saying anything,
even in my mangled
fractured English,
I am imagining him,
imagining and wishing
and hoping

that he is safe.
Hoping,
I'm starting to think,
might be the bravest thing a person can do.

PART FOUR
Hoping

I.

It is early in the morning,
    the sun has not yet fully risen,
    and I am sitting at the kitchen table.

    The buttery smell of blueberry muffins
    that are baking
    wafts through the kitchen.
    I love these mornings with Aunt Michelle.
    We don't always talk,
    sometimes we just listen to
    the quiet French music she likes,
    flip through the newspaper together,
    be together.

    Today, though, I have a mission.
    My pencil hovers above the paper.
    It is not that I have forgotten how to write in Arabic,
    but sometimes my hand needs to wake up to it again.

    This is my fifth letter to Fatima.

She has not written back once.
I try to tell myself it is because
she is busy,
because she has always been
more of a talker than a writer.
I don't let myself think about
the other possibilities
the scary reasons
for why I haven't heard from her.

In my letters, I have told her about America—
about the creaky old house I live in,
about Mrs. Ravenswood's ESL class,
about the boy in my math class who always wears
space shirts
and has messy brown hair.

But this letter is different.
In this letter, I am telling her about Issa
and how we don't know where he is,
or if he's okay.

I am begging for Fatima to answer me
because I've convinced myself that
if she can tell me some happy news from back home,
everything will be okay.
If she tells me something happy,

I will be able to believe that
somehow Issa is happy too.
That he is safe.

That is so impressive, Aunt Michelle says.
What? I ask, looking up from the lined page of
notebook paper.
*That you can write in two languages. I wish Sarah knew how
to speak Arabic.*
I shrug.
In America,
I have picked up a habit of shrugging.

I don't write that well in English, I say because
I don't know what to say about Sarah.
I never know what to say about Sarah.

Aunt Michelle slides down into the seat beside me.
She smells like sugar and flour.

I wish your uncle would teach her. But he hasn't.
I still don't know what to say.
I press the point of my pencil into the paper.
He seems busy
is all I manage.

Aunt Michelle gives me a sad smile.

179

I think it's more than that.
But she doesn't say anything else.

I think again of that Arabic proverb:
He cannot give what he does not have.

Aunt Michelle gets up to check on the muffins
and I go back to writing to Fatima.
I end my letter with telling her about the school play.

Can you believe it?
My American school has a play that I can try out for.
Do you think I should try out?
I wish you were here.
We could do it together.
I miss doing everything
together.

II.

I'm with Mama at the doctor's office,
    and we are holding our breath
    as the ultrasound technician squeezes gel
    out over Mama's round stomach
    and then presses the wand against it.

    The screen overhead lights up,
    a tangle of gray and black shadows
    that at first don't look like anything,
    but then, if you squint your eyes just right,
    you see
    a foot
    a hand
    a mouth.

    You see
    life.

    The room explodes with a sound
    like the gallop of horse feet.

It is the sound of
one
tiny
loud
miracle.

Do you want to know what you're having? the technician
asks Mama.
Mama turns to me.
Her English has been getting better from the lessons
she's been taking at the mosque,
but it is still not so good.

Aren't I having a baby? Mama says to me in Arabic.
I laugh.
The woman looks at me,
confused.

I tell her what Mama said,
a shy smile on my face.
The woman laughs,
and this makes Mama smile
wide.
She has made an American
laugh.

Back home, Mama always made us

laugh.
She wasn't funny in the way Issa was.
Issa's funny is like an elephant,
impossible to miss,
you know when he wants to make you
laugh.

But Mama's funny is more like a cat,
slinking around,
hiding out in corners,
brushing up on you by surprise.

Mama, with her perfectly wrapped scarf
her clean nails
her gentle way of walking on the ground
does not seem like she would have a sharp tongue,
which makes the fact she is funny,
even funnier.

I can tell this ultrasound technician did not expect
Mama to be funny.
I think she did not know what to expect from us at all.
But when she smiles and asks, *Does she want to know if the*
baby is a boy
or a girl?
I know she likes us
more than she thought she would.

I translate for Mama,
even though the wet look in her eyes
lets me know she already understood.
Mama nods,
and the woman presses the wand back down on
Mama's stomach.
She says she thinks she knows, but wants to take
just one more look
to be sure.

It is important to be certain about these things, she says.
The wand moves in circles on Mama's tummy
and I go back to holding my breath.

As I thought, the technician says,
smiling,
another little girl.

Bint, I confirm to Mama.
Her eyes spill over,
tears running down her cheeks that have grown fuller
in the months we have been here.

Pressure builds behind my eyes,
too.
Mama grabs my hands,
squeezes.

I'd almost forgotten that it's possible
to cry because of
happiness.

III.

I hold Mama's hand as we walk out of the hospital.
    We are both in a daze,
    the word *bint* on our lips,
    tasting like chocolate,
    tasting like afternoon mint tea with three extra
    spoonfuls of sugar,
    tasting like sunshine.

Tasting like hope.

    The lobby of the hospital is decorated for Christmas,
    a large tree glistening with lights,
    branches with pine cones draped
    across the nurses' desks.
    "Jingle Bells" plays over the speakers;
    a song that I had not heard until two weeks ago,
    but I now know
    every
    single
    word

and I don't think I'll ever forget
any of them.

There is so much happiness and cheer
and for a moment,
I feel that Mama and I are part of it too.
It feels like a party we were invited to,
not one that we are watching through a window.

But then, right as we are walking out
of the hospital doors,
a woman stops us.
Hey! she says, pointing a finger at Mama's face.
Hey! she repeats, the word like a stone thrown,

You don't have to wear that anymore.

The cold air from outside hisses in through the
half-opened door, and it no
longer feels festive.

Her finger moves from Mama's face to
point to her head,
to her hijab.
*You're in America now. You're
free.*

Mama does not say anything;
she grips my hand.
The woman looks from Mama
to me
and back at Mama.
Do you speak English?

The snake of fear
uncoils in my stomach.
I am frozen for a moment
and then I urge Mama
through the door,
squeezing past the woman,
stepping closer to the outside,
to the cold.

As I pass the woman, my shoulder inches from
her chest,
I say,
Excuse us. Thank you. We are
happy.

I do not know why I say that.
My English words are all mumbled,
and I'm not sure she heard me,
or that she understood.
But I wanted her to understand

that we're happy here,
even if we don't look like what she thinks of
as happy.

Outside, sleet is
falling from the sky.
Mama has not let go of my hand.
We are happy, I say again, whispering it into the cold air.
Saying it to Mama,
to the baby.

The baby girl who will be
born here,
but who is loved on both sides of the ocean.

We are, Mama says,
and there are new tears in her eyes.

IV.

It is winter break
  and I do not have school for two
  whole
  weeks.

  I am planning to use
  all my free time
  to pick out a monologue
  for my play audition
  and then practice it
  over and over again.

  Why don't they call it Christmas break?
  I ask Aunt Michelle one morning
  when I am sitting in the kitchen,
  eating the almond-flour pancakes
  with cacao nibs that she has made.
  I had never heard of a cacao nib before
  Aunt Michelle.

Cacao nibs,
I have learned,
are a healthier version of a chocolate chip,
a little less delicious,
but I pretend to love them because
it makes Aunt Michelle happy.

Aunt Michelle laughs at my question and adds
more berries to my plate.
I am amazed that even though
the ground outside is frozen solid,
we are able to eat as many berries as we want.

Because, habibti—
Aunt Michelle has recently started calling me that.
It is an Arabic word that
she has heard Uncle Mazin say
over and over.
There is something funny about hearing that word
come out of her mouth.
There is something lovely about it.

There are other holidays this time of year too.
Like Hanukkah and
Kwanzaa.

I nod and I am about to ask more questions

about these holidays that I have never heard of,
when my cousin Sarah comes clomping
into the kitchen,
her fuzzy pink slippers pounding against the tile.

Sarah walks with purpose,
like she is not afraid of being heard.
She has that same American boldness
that I've seen advertised on billboards,
like the restaurant down the street
that brags about their
fully
loaded
special
that comes with everything,
but really only includes
peppers, onions, and cheese.

I've decided it is very American
to have the audacity
to claim that three things
add up to everything.

Sarah's black hair,
the only part of her that clearly came from my uncle
is tangled with sleep
and she yawns as Aunt Michelle pushes a plate in front
    of her.

She cranes to look outside at the backyard.
Good, she says. *It snowed.*
She forks a piece of pancake into her mouth,
and makes a face.
Can't you ever make normal pancakes, Mom?
Aunt Michelle casts me a smile and I feel like
we are sharing a secret since I helped her pick out
the almond flour recipe,
helped her count out the cacao nibs.

Can you drop me off at Mount Storm Park later?
Aunt Michelle pauses, the faucet still on,
dripping water onto the dirty pancake skillet.
You're going sledding?
Sarah nods and in between bites mumbles
the names of her friends all together
MinaHarperSloane as if they are one inseparable unit.

Sure. Aunt Michelle tosses the dish towel
that is seasonally patterned
with snowflakes over her shoulder.
Mama never used to change the décor
simply because the weather did,
but Aunt Michelle seems to rearrange
the whole house just because of the thermostat.

Sarah stands up and Aunt Michelle says,
Jude should go with you,

and I know from the tone of her voice it is a command
not a suggestion.

I am expecting Sarah to push back,
to argue,
to clomp clomp clomp her slippers all over the floor.

But instead, she says,
Okay, with a shrug and then turns to me and says,
Just don't be weird.

I know I should feel stung,
but the sound of the thrilling
okay
is so much louder in my head than
weird.

V.

Before I know it, I am riding in Aunt Michelle's car
  up, up, up
  a steep hill to Mount Storm Park.

I am bundled in a coat that I have borrowed from
Sarah because Aunt Michelle said
that my new beautiful coat
was not warm enough for sledding.

The coat is powder blue and puffy
and so warm that I am sweating by the time
we get to the park.
We wave good-bye to Aunt Michelle
and as we walk over to Sarah's friends,
she says again,
Don't be weird.
And then she adds,
Like your friend is.

I know she is talking about Layla

and a metallic taste gathers in my mouth,
a warning.

I feign ignorance and ask, *Which friend?*
Um, Sarah says. She tugs on the ends of her hat,
which looks like a wool bonnet
but somehow still seems stylish.
The one who wears—

Layla, I say,
What is so—I pause and then try the decidedly
American word—*weird*
about her?
Sarah waves at Harper, who has just jumped out of her
mom's shiny silver minivan
and says, *She just acts like she isn't from here, you know?*
All the warmth that had built up in me during the car
ride rushes out of my body
and I shiver inside the blue puffy coat.

But— I think and my mind
floods with all those thoughts
that I try my best to keep at bay,
that are like wolves in the night,
howling that I am not from here,
that I don't belong here,
that I will never belong here.

Layla's American, is all I mean to say.
She was born here, I add because I can't help myself. *She's
    American.*
But Sarah is already walking toward Harper
toward Mina
toward Sloane

and I am trudging behind her,
trying to figure out how not to act weird,
trying to figure out how to belong.

VI.

We are on the top of the tallest hill
and SarahMinaHarperSloane are talking about
tryouts for the school play
and I am planning to just listen but
then something inside of me kicks.
An impulse that I have
buried and thought I left on the other side of the
Atlantic.
I was at that meeting too, I spit out.

Sarah gives me a look and I know it is a warning.
Mina says, *Are you thinking of trying out?*
But the way she says it
does not sound like a question,
more like a joke.

Layla worked on the sets last year, I say, and I know
my English words are difficult to understand because
when I get nervous my accent gets thicker
and I also think the fact that my feet are
freezing is not helping matters.

It is hard to think
in two languages
when your feet are freezing.

Another warning glare from Sarah who is sitting on
her sled impatiently waiting to glide down the hill
but I can tell she is nervous to leave her
weird
cousin with her friends.

I want to work on the sets, Harper offers.
Harper reminds me of Auntie Amal—agreeable and
friendly.
Who is Layla?

She's in eighth grade, I say.
We don't know many eighth graders, Mina says.
Is she the one that— Sloane asks, but does not finish.
Sarah is looking at me to answer.

Layla is the one who worked on
the sets, I say, that impulse kick-kick-kicking
inside of me, urging me to remember who I was,
not a girl who held her tongue,
but Jude who was always told, *Skety.*
A girl who promised her older brother she would be
    brave.

I look out at the snowy hills
that are glistening in the afternoon light
and I think about how badly
I wish my older brother were here.

How badly I need to know
that someday I am going
to have the chance to tell him
about the day I went sledding
with four Americans.

Missing Issa has become
a physical ache inside of me,
like a rotting cavity that is growing
more painful every day.

Everyone stares at me in
silence
until finally Mina
and then Sarah
followed by Sloane
volunteer that they are planning to try out
but they all downplay their chances
talking about how seventh graders never get
cast in actual speaking roles
and definitely
never get any

of the parts with singing solos
except for a girl
named Abigail last year who got one
and this year she'll probably get a lead role.

I am going to try out, I say, making sure my English is
as precise and clear as it can be
so that they can understand me,
perfectly.

Sarah's eyes meet mine, but I meet hers back
like I am daring her to slide down the hill
that I have already gone down.

VII.

You can't try out, Layla says
 as the steam from the bowl of lentil soup
 wafts up to her face.
 Her mother has ladled us two big bowls of soup
 convinced that
 the lemon in the broth will stave off
 all the winter viruses going around.

 We don't want you to lose your voice
 before your tryout, Layla's mom says to me, because
 even she has heard the news.

 Everyone has heard the news,
 except for Mama because
 I don't know how to tell her.

 My mom isn't mad about it, Layla says,
 spooning hot soup into her mouth,
 and swallowing with a slurp.
 Her swallow is a big fat period

at the end of her sentence,
a declaration.
She just thinks it's strange because you know, you—

There is a long break.
I have learned Americans love to say *you know* and then
stop
talking.
They force you to fill in the hard parts,
the things they are not brave enough to say.

I shake my head and think of that baby
that is growing inside of
Mama's belly, that kicks and kicks
just like the spirit inside of me has once again started to
kick and kick.

She doesn't need to know now,
which is what I say when I mean,
I'm not sure she would understand
and
I don't want to upset her when she has that baby inside
of her,
but also
I am not going to say, you know, *and make you*
fill in all the tough stuff.

Layla tears a piece of pita bread in half
and then tells me all of the other reasons she thinks
I shouldn't try out.

You don't speak English, she says.
I frown, and in perfect—thank you very much—
English, say back,
I do, too.

You know what I mean, she says again,
and this time I say,
*No, I do not know. You're going to have to
tell me.*

So she tells me that my English is good
but it isn't *like native speaker English good*
and the tryouts are so competitive,
even kids who have been acting
for years don't get a part,
and can I even sing?
And what will I use as my monologue?
Can I even memorize something in English?

So many questions,
so many doubts.
When I don't say anything, she frowns.
*I'm not trying to be mean. I'm trying to be
realistic.*

Layla, I say, and I hardly ever say her name
so that catches her attention. *I left home, I flew
across an ocean.*
My brother is missing,
in the middle of a war zone.
What is there left to be afraid of?

She gives me that look again.
The one that makes me feel like there is something
behind me, something around the corner.

There is always something to be afraid of, she insists.
And I know she is right,
I know more than she thinks I do.

But still I say,
I'm choosing not to be afraid.
I say it more for me,
more for Issa,
than for Layla.
The words are a wish,
a prayer.

I lean forward, putting my elbows on the table,
the way I used to watch Baba do,
the way I watched Issa do.
The way people do when they want
to make sure you see them,

that you know they're claiming
their space.

Jude, those parts aren't for girls like us.

What do you mean?

We're the type of girls that design the sets,
that stay backstage.
We're not girls who
glow in the spotlight.

I take another bite of the soup
and it tastes like home,
it tastes like the future.

But I want to be, I say.

She gives me a look,
not *the* look,
it is a look that I have never seen before.

She is seeing me differently.
She is seeing
me.

VIII.

From the moment
 I heard Mrs. Bloom say
 that for the tryout
 we would need a monologue
 and a song,
 I knew what song
 I would sing.

 Some of my strongest memories
 of my brother
 are him standing up on the couch,
 belting out the words to
 Whitney Houston's "I Will Always Love You,"
 while Fatima and I ate our *asroneyeh*
 and sang along with him.
 Our mouths full of food
 and laughter
 and love.

 I practice my singing in the upstairs room

when Mama is at the mosque
or when she is downstairs
pestering Uncle Mazin
about why the thermostat
never stays at the temperature
at which she set it.

Some of the first English words I ever learned
were from "I Will Always Love You."
Issa would hop from couch cushion
to couch cushion
singing the chorus,
declaring his undying love,
his smile so bright
it made us squint.

Now when I sing the song
I see the ghost of all the days
my brother has been missing
line up in front of me.

I stare them down
as I sing as loud as I can
about the strength
of my love.

It is a hard song

to sing without the music
to accompany it.

I know I should choose something else,
something easier,
but my heart won't let me.

When I sing it,
alone in the upstairs room,
staring at those old plaster beige walls
that are becoming more and more
familiar,
I do not feel like I am
singing it alone.

I hear my brother's voice
in my head,
filling in the melody.

IX.

It takes me a long time to choose my monologue.
    Aunt Michelle watches all my favorite movies with me,
    and Sarah watches too.
    She won't tell either of us
    what monologue she has chosen
    and sometimes I wonder if that is because
    she is scared that I might steal it.
    Which would mean she is nervous about me trying out,
    and not because she thinks it will be embarrassing,
    but because she is worried I might be
    good.

    This is probably not
    true, but I like to tell myself it anyway.

    In all my favorite movies,
    the actresses speak fast,
    and people speak right back to them,
    no pauses.

It is hard to find a monologue,
it is hard to find a place
where my favorite actresses are allowed
to speak without a man
interrupting them before their full thought
has been spoken.

But finally, I pick one.
It comes from *Notting Hill,*
which is not my favorite Julia Roberts movie,
but it was one of Fatima's because it is more dramatic
and romantic
than it is funny.

I pick the part
where her character is explaining
that her life
has not been as charmed
as everyone at the dinner party thinks
it has been.

I have never been a famous actress
with a seemingly glamorous life
that people on the outside
think is perfect.

But I have lived a life that people don't quite

understand
in a place that lots of people, I am learning, don't
understand
at all.

I lean into that feeling,
of insecurity,
but also of the boldness
of surprising people.

It is not lost on me that in my monologue
I am pretending to be a famous actress,
I am pretending to be grown-up.

I am pretending.

I practice the English words in the mirror,
I watch the scene over and over
and over
and over
again.

I try to make my mouth move
just like Julia Roberts's does.
My big mouth,
my mouth that I sometimes
like to think looks like Julia Roberts's,

my mouth that sometimes says things that surprise me,
that surprise others.

Every time I practice,
I think about how wonderful
it feels to speak
for two whole minutes,
with no fear of being interrupted,
with no one saying, *Skety*.

Just me and my big mouth,
speaking,
being heard.

X.

The day before my tryout, I
    decide to write to Fatima again.
    She has not answered a single letter of mine,
    which would make me angry
    if I let myself think about it too much.
    So I don't.

    I rustle around in the room I share with Mama,
    looking for my pencils and paper,
    looking for stamps and envelopes.

    It's during this rustling,
    I find the stack of envelopes,
    barely hidden under the bed,
    as if whoever
    stashed them there
    didn't want them to be found,
    but didn't make too much effort
    to disguise their existence.

I recognize the handwriting immediately.
It is poised and neat,
because I am confident in the Arabic alphabet,
unlike my shaky form when it comes to English letters.

The envelopes are bound together with a silk ribbon,
the kind Mama uses to tie back her hair,
and a thought springs into my head.
I try to push it away,
but it keeps growing
and growing.

I race downstairs and find Mama
in the chair in the living room near the big window
where she often sits during the day,
looking out the window,
looking like she is waiting for something.

I hold the envelopes out to her
and even though
I can see her swollen belly
under the cream-colored blanket
she has wrapped around herself,
I cannot tame my anger.

You said you sent them,
I say as tears run down my face.

You promised.
She pulls me down beside her,
but I continue to hold out the envelopes.
They hover in the air like a question mark.

Will you sing your song for me?
Hearing my mama say that catches me
off guard
because it means she knows,
she knows about the song,
which means she knows about the tryout,
which
means
she
knows
I
didn't
tell her.

And this is so
so
surprising
that I almost don't notice that
Mama made this declaration,
this request,
in English.

You know about the tryout,

I say, in English as well.
A'arf, she says.
She holds me close
and I feel each pulse of her stomach,
small promises of what is to come.

Mama is wearing a cozy sweater and cotton pants that
are stretchy but elegant.
I have never seen her wear a sweater or pants,
and I know Aunt Michelle
must've bought them for her,
and that's when I realize
America
has also changed Mama. I just haven't
been paying close enough attention.

Why? I want to know.
Why didn't you send the letters?
Why didn't you confront me about the play?
Why does our family keep so many secrets?

She strokes the back of my head like she used to do
when I was little and how I know she will do
to my baby sister once she is old enough to sit.

She tells me that Auntie Amal and Fatima
were forced to move from our town
because Fatima's baba

lost his job.
Business is bad, she says, and I see so much
sadness in her eyes.
People are scrambling for jobs.

Where did they go? I ask.

Lebanon. There is not much there,
but people say it is doing better than other places.

Other places
being our city.

She has not heard from Auntie Amal
since they moved.
She does not know if they are okay,
but she is choosing to believe that they are because
Allah would want us to have faith.

I didn't want you to worry.
You are too young to carry so
much worry.

I know she is thinking of Issa
and how our worry about him is so big,
it is eating us both up inside.
I know she is trying to tell me

that she didn't think I could handle
any more worry on top of that,
but I am trying to show her that here in America,
I am growing up.

She pulls me even closer to her
which I know is her way of asking me *Why?*
It is her turn to ask me about my
secret,
secrets.

I didn't want you to worry, I say,
half joking
half serious.

She laughs a little and kisses the top of my head.
Will you sing your song for me? she asks,
again.

I begin the song slowly,
it feels so strange to sing those words aloud,
here,
in this chair,
in America,
with Mama,
so far away from Issa.

She must feel it too because I sense the recognition
in the way her body curls around mine
like it isn't only holding me,
but it's also holding
a memory.

XI.

On the day of tryouts,
    there are so many people in the auditorium
    and all of them have racing hearts and sweaty palms.
    There is enough energy in here to power a train,
    an airplane,
    a small country.

    Layla has come with me even though
    she is not trying out.
    You don't have to do this, she says.
    She is more nervous than I am
    and she doesn't even have to get up on that big stage
    with the blinding lights.

    Maybe that is why she is more nervous than me
    because she is the kind of person who does not
    want to stand under a blinding light.

    I sometimes wish I was like that.
    That I was happy to blend in,
    fade into the background.

I sometimes worry that there is something
wrong with me that
I so badly want to know that other people
see me.

But then I think about all the other people,
all the other people who are in this room right now
for the exact same reason,
and realize my want,
my dream,
is as big and real
and valid as theirs.

I spot Sarah in the auditorium
and HarperSloaneMina sitting a few rows ahead of us.
They seem nervous too, grasping at each other's arms,
bumping elbows for luck.

One by one,
we walk onto the stage,
we recite our monologue,
we sing our song.

One by one,
we are told
thank you,
and dismissed offstage.
When Mrs. Bloom calls my name,

I can tell that she knows
how to pronounce my first name
but is unsure what to do with my last.
She skips over my last name,
gargling all the letters together,
making a mess of the name that is mine
Baba's
Issa's
and will be my baby sister's.

And for a moment,
my nerves turn from anxious
to angry,
from nervous
to defiant.

I walk out onto the stage,
and do not squint in the bright light
but instead stare right back at it.

I am going to give her,
give everyone,
a reason to know how to say my name,
my full name.

I open my mouth
and start to sing.

XII.

It happens while
    I am waiting
    for the results
    of the tryouts to be posted.

Your body is growing up,
Mama tells me
in a soft voice
when she sees the tears in my eyes
and the fear on my face
as I look at the bloodstained spots
that appeared on our sheets
overnight.

Initially I thought the blood had come
from Mama
and I cried for the baby.
But then I saw the
slow
thick

crimson drip
between my legs,
and I felt the dense cramp of my stomach
and I knew.

I bit my lip,
afraid of what this meant,
afraid of what it meant was
coming.

But Mama held me and told me that
I might be growing up
but I don't need to be afraid
because even if she has a tiny baby in her stomach
I'll always be her baby too.

And when she held me,
I could feel that there was still space in her arms
for me.

XIII.

Mama does not ask about it,
　　but when I unpack
　　those scarves I buried in my suitcase
　　she smiles,
　　tears in her eyes.

I pick a scarf that is turquoise,
the color of the sea in the summer when the sun hits it
at the exact right angle.

Mama and I fold the square scarf into a triangle,
and Mama helps me drape it onto my head,
crossing the corners of it around my neck,
and gently pinning the tails of the scarf in place.

We stand together in front of the mirror
to admire the result.
My face looks older.
Different.

Maybe it is a trick of the light,
maybe it is the beautiful scarf,
but I feel like I look wiser,
like someone I would ask for advice,
not someone asking for it.

You are a woman, Jude, Mama says,
her voice equal parts
awe and admiration.

I am looking into the mirror
at the image of me that I do not recognize.
A stranger who I will
get to know.

A stranger who I am
excited to meet.

PART FIVE
Growing

I.

We call Baba on Skype
   so that he can see me.
   The new me.

I hear his gasp through the computer
as he takes in the image in front of him.
His baby girl who no longer looks like
a baby.
His other baby girl who is getting ready
to be born.

I twirl around,
partly to be silly,
partly to avoid seeing the sadness
in Baba's eyes,
as he watches us and takes in all he is missing.

Have you heard from Issa? I ask,
even though I know the answer.
But it feels wrong not to ask.

Sometimes I feel like you have to say things out loud
just to remind the universe
that you're still thinking about them.

Baba shakes his head,
his eyes downcast.
But when his eyes meet mine again,
there is a spark of hope.

Look at you, Jude, habibti,
so grown-up, he says.
I'm proud and your brother would be too.

My heart swells up with aching,
longing,
but it swells up with love, too.

II.

Everyone has a reaction to my hijab,
   like Layla's mother who gently
   grabs both my hands
   and pulls me close to her,
   kissing me on each cheek and
   greeting me like I am a brand-new person.

And then there are the people on the street
   who never used to notice me
   before when I glided down Ludlow
   in my beautiful coat
   but now stop and turn their heads,
   their eyes watching me like
   I am a ticking time bomb.

Or there is Aunt Michelle who
   pulls me aside and asks me if
   I really want to wear it
   and I look beautiful no matter what
   but she hopes I know it is my choice.

No matter how many times I explain to her
that of course it is my choice
and this is something I have been waiting for,
she still casts a look at Mama,
like she is a detective
who is going to get to the bottom of the
case
when really there is nothing to solve,
only something to be happy about,
something that back home,
would've been greeted like Layla's mother greeted me,
like a celebration,
a blessing.

I know Aunt Michelle
means well,
and that she has just heard the stories,
the same ones that I have heard,
about girls from countries nearby mine
who are forced to dress a certain way,
forced to act a certain way.

But I want to explain to Aunt Michelle that
this,
my choice,
is not like that thing,
that thing that she doesn't quite

know how to say.
That thing that she's afraid of.

That thing that Americans often say
you know about and wait
awkwardly
for you
to fill in the blank.

That thing that also makes me angry,
as angry as it makes them.
I want women like Aunt Michelle
to understand
that it is not only women who look like them
who are free
who think
and care about other women.

That it is possible for two things to look
similar
but be completely different.

That I cover my head like other
strong
respected
women have done before me,
like Malala Yousafzai

like Kariman Abuljadayel
like my mama.

That I cover my head
not because I am ashamed
forced
or hiding.

But because I am
proud
and want to seen
as I am.

III.

Mrs. Ravenswood
    is one of the only Americans
    who doesn't act
    suspicious of my headscarf.

    When I walk into
    her classroom
    the first day
    that my head is covered,
    she smiles at me,
    looking me right in the
    eyes,
    seeing me.

    Hello, Jude,
    she says.
    Good morning.
    You look nice
    today.

There is an Arabic proverb that says:
She makes you feel
like a loaf of freshly baked bread.

It is said about
the nicest
kindest
people.
The type of people
who help you
rise.

IV.

The day the results of the tryouts are posted
    the news spreads through the halls like water
    that has burst from a dam.

    We all run, run,
    run
    to see the simple white paper
    with simple black letters
    that has been hung in the window of the library.

    Layla has beat me to the paper
    and I see her in the crowd of bodies
    shouldering to get a look.

    People are talking all around me,
    Abigail Beth Malone is whispered with reverence
    and I know she is the eighth grader
    who last year as a seventh grader
    snagged a talking part in the musical.

For a moment,
I am jealous of her,
not just because she has won the role of Belle
of the beauty
of the star
but because her name already sounds like the name
of a famous actress
whereas I have a name that people
struggle to pronounce.

But the sour taste of jealousy,
its acidic tang in my mouth
fades
the moment Layla rushes over to me
and squeezes my shoulder.
You got a part!

She shouts so loud that people
turn their heads to look at us
two hijabi girls
standing in the middle of the hallway
in the middle of America
celebrating.

V.

I have been cast as Plumette,
    the feather duster,
    which is not a big role,
    but it is a role,
    which is all that matters.

    Sarah has made it
    but she is only in the chorus
    as is Sloane
    and Harper and Mina did not make it
    but were offered positions for tech crew
    if they want them,
    but Sarah thinks only Harper will
    work on the sets.

    Mina doesn't want to make sets, she sneers,
    and I know she is talking about Layla,
    turning her nose up at my friend.

    But really Sarah is just mad

that my role
is bigger
than hers,
which is something I don't think she ever thought
would happen, which is something I never
thought would happen.

I remember the acidic tang in my mouth
when I first learned
Abigail Beth Malone
with her movie star name would be the lead
and I try to be patient with Sarah
and forgive her for not being happy
for me.

Sarah has never commented on my headscarf
but on Saturday afternoon
when her
and me
and Aunt Michelle
are all watching the movie *Beauty and the Beast*
a movie I have never seen
but am already falling in love with—

Sarah says,
Plumette is supposed to be sexy.
I don't think they will let you wear that

during the musical.
She stares at me,
her gaze is a challenge.

She is asking me to choose
between two things
without realizing it is her
and people like her
that think you have to choose.

The day after the cast list was posted
I saw Mrs. Bloom in the hall
and she touched my elbow and said,
You are our Plumette because I can tell you have
punch, my dear,
liters of it.

I don't know what Mrs. Bloom quite meant by punch,
but I tell that to Sarah,
and she says, *Or because you have a thick accent*
so you won't have to even
fake that part.

And I know I should feel angry at Sarah,
but I don't.
Not really.

Mostly, I feel sorry for myself
because Sarah is right that I do
have a thick accent
and I wonder if everyone else in the cast
thinks the same thing she does.
My skin feels hot and too thin
all at the same time.

But then I remember it doesn't matter,
I have a role!
I'm in the play!
And I have this magical thing called
punch.

Liters of it.

VI.

Mrs. Bloom tells us that the most successful plays
    are successful because the cast
    and crew
    become like one big family,
    all working toward the same goal.

    She separates us
    into groups of four,
    each group a mix
    of actors
    chorus members
    set design
    and tech crew.

    Jude, right?
    the boy from my math class says.
    The one with the dark messy hair
    and the galaxy-patterned T-shirts.
    I'm Miles.

I look at his shirt.
It's black with
a photograph of
the full moon.

Miles.
His name makes me
smile because
it is not
a name I've heard
before.

And as he answers
the first "icebreaker" question—
an American term
I have just learned,
but am already really fond of—
I temporarily forget about
all the miles between me
and home.

Cool, another girl
in our group says.
Her hair is a tangle of
red curls and she is chewing gum
even though I'm pretty sure
we aren't allowed to chew gum
inside the auditorium.

I'm Ruth.
I work on sets.
And I'm really excited
about this year's play
because musicals are kind
of my whole life
and I can't wait to move to
New York City
when I'm older.

The other person
in our group
is Ethan.
He is playing the role
of the Beast
and we all act like
he is a
real
life
movie star
even though he has
a small piece of granola bar
stuck in his braces.

I think I want to be an actor
when I grow up
but my dad
doesn't exactly love

that idea, he says.

My heart pinches
when he says this.
It makes me think
of Issa and Baba
and how hard
it can be when
what you want
runs against a different
current
from your father.

I wonder if
when
Issa comes home,
Baba and him
will fight less.
If how much
they've missed each other
will be enough to build
a bridge across all
their differences.

Mrs. Bloom calls out
that it is time for a break
and Ethan quickly moves

in the direction of
Abigail Beth Malone
and the other eighth-grade stars.

Ruth takes off toward
the edge of the stage
where a lot of set design kids
including Layla
have gathered
and are combing through
a packet of paint swatches.

Miles, though,
he doesn't run off.
Are you okay? he asks me.
He looks at me like
he is seeing all my thoughts
about Issa and Baba.

I'm okay, I say quietly.
I was just thinking.

He shoves his hands
into his black, baggy pants.
*That's cool. I also
like thinking.*

I laugh a little,
which makes him smile,
which makes me think again
about how Miles is a pretty good
antidote for miles.

So what do you think
it would feel like to step on the moon?
he asks.

I blink.
At first, I think I misunderstood him.
That something is wrong with my translation.

You know, he says,
and I see a flash of embarrassment
cross over his face.
It's something to
think about.

Mrs. Bloom announces
that we have one more
minute left of our break.

I hear the crinkling of
potato chip bags
and the shuffling of

sneakers.

My mind feels gummy
as I search for an
answer to his
question.

Words swim through my head,
but I am unable to catch any of them.
Fragments of phrases in Arabic,
crumbs of English.

Free, I say, even though it's not really what I mean.
How do I put into words what I think it would be like
to stand on a rock
in the middle of a black expanse?
To look down at our world
and see it with new eyes?
To feel so tiny
and so big
all at the same time?

He studies me for a moment,
and I worry he is going to laugh,
that he will think
what I said was dumb,
but instead his face breaks into a wide smile.

251

Yeah, me too.

Yeah, me too
are now my three favorite words in English.

VII.

Some days
   I still feel lost in the halls of school.
   I know where I am going
   but I can't shake the feeling that I won't,
   that I don't,
   belong in whatever classroom I end up in.

   But whenever I walk
   into Mrs. Ravenwood's
   I feel safe.
   I feel at
   home.

   Ben is teaching us all
   new American slang
   words that he has learned.

   Bougie, he says.
   Means fancy.
   Rich.

Boogie? Omar says,
he pretends to dance
and then laughs.
Omar has a laugh
Like Issa's.
It makes you want to
join in.

No, Ben says,
even though now
he is laughing too.
Boo-Gee.

We all repeat after Ben,
the new word tasting
like America
on our lips.

VIII.

Play practices
    start running later
    and later.

So late that most nights
Mrs. Bloom orders dinner
for us and we take a break
halfway through to eat

I usually eat with Layla
and her set design friends,
but today I go a grab a seat
beside Miles,
even though
Layla has told me she thinks
he's *weird*
with his black T-shirts with pictures
of planets and his baggy black pants
and black combat boots.

But I think Miles is interesting
with his facts about space
and his theories about extraterrestrial life
and his voice that is soft but solid
like rain on a roof.

We are all eating pizza again,
for the fourth night in a row,
because the school has some arrangement
with a local pizza place.
I would eat pizza one hundred nights in a row
and still be happy,
I say to Miles as I grab another slice of cheese pizza.

He makes a funny sound.
I am learning that Miles doesn't really laugh
so much as he smiles with his eyes to let you know
he agrees with you.

Did you eat a lot of pizza back in . . . ?
He trails off.
Syria, I fill in for him,
and briefly wonder if he forgot the name of my country
or was too afraid to say it.
Either answer makes me a tiny bit sad.

There were a couple of places that sold pizza, I say,

pausing to take another bite of my slice,
the oozy greasy cheese
sliding down the back of my throat.
But they were expensive, mostly for tourists.
My family didn't really eat there.

I watch him studying me again
and all of a sudden,
my skin feels paper-thin,
like he can see right through me.

I worry that he is eyeing my hijab,
and deciding that I am too different,
for him to want to be friends anymore.

But then he says, *I just think it's so cool,*
That you've lived this whole other life.
The most exciting thing I've ever done
is taken my dog on a walk by myself
at the park after dark.
Totally boring, right?

I laugh.
He thinks I'm cool!
A tiny voice inside of me shouts
and my heart does a victory dance.

You have a dog? I ask.
Yeah. His name is Sputnik. Named after the space—

Satellite. I finish his sentence.

Right, he says.
his eyes doing that smile-laugh thing again,
and now my skin feels thin but in a good way
like it's more open to the universe.

He tells me about Sputnik,
how she has black and white fur
and her favorite thing in the world is to chase squirrels.

Did you have a dog? he asks.
I shake my head,
and just when I'm about to explain that
it's not because I don't like dogs
I just actually don't know much about dogs
because no one back home had one,
Mrs. Bloom claps her hands,
bringing us all to attention.

Let's get back to it, Mrs. Bloom says,
And I give Miles a small wave as I head back up
toward the stage
to rehearse

because I have a role
in my American school's play.

IX.

When Layla rushes over to me,
    on Valentine's Day
    I think she is going to share some gossip
    and I fill with anticipation.

    I have secretly been holding out hope
    that someone would slide a card into my locker,
    a chocolate,
    or a rose.
    And whenever I imagined this,
    it was always the same person,
    with his black T-shirts
    and black pants
    and black boots.

    But my locker is empty
    all that is there is Layla
    whose face is filled with sadness
    and twisted with worry.

And then she tells me:
About the explosion,
about the blood in the streets,
and the horror
and the death.

I am upset and sad about what she tells me,
but confused why she is so fixated on this news
when it happened in a city
so far away from us.

Be careful, Jude, she says,
and I don't understand.
She tells me that now I will learn what it means to be a
Muslim
in America.

X.

I shrug off Layla's warning,
    because in America,
    I have perfected the shrug.
    Because in America,
    I have come to believe that things
    work out.
    Because in America,
    I have been cast in a play,
    and in America,
    I have become friends with a cute boy
    who wears T-shirts with the moon on them.

    I do not believe her.
    I do not want to believe her,
    but soon I come to understand,
    as the glances shot in my direction
    turn from slightly unsure
    to plainly hostile.

    Each glare demanding an apology
    an explanation

for something
I did not do.

That afternoon,
I walk home from school
because we do not have play practice
and I notice a man
who is standing on the corner waiting for the bus.
I give him a small smile,
but he does not smile back.

I look down at the ground,
ready to be on my way,
when I hear the shoes
pounding on the pavement behind me.

I glance over my shoulder
and see that the man is following me.
My heart jumps up in my chest,
and it hammers furiously.

Go back to where you came from, he says.
We don't want you here.

There is a ringing in my ears
and for a moment I freeze,
unsure I actually heard
what I heard.

I want to say something
to make this man understand
that he has no reason to be afraid of me,
to hate me,
but all I manage to do is walk away.

The ringing in my ears stays for a little while,
dulling from a sharp scream
to a softer echo.
I walk up the hill toward what is now my home.
That's when I hear a familiar voice.

Jude!

I jump from the surprise.
Then I turn and there is Miles.
He is panting and his face is flushed from the cold air.

I saw what happened.
I didn't know what to do.
I'm so sorry.

I hang my head.
Somehow it feels worse that Miles saw.

Jude, he says, looking at me.
That guy is a jerk.

He squints up at the sun.
It is a funny thing,
how a day can be so bright,
but so cold.

I'm sorry, he says again.
His words are jumbled
and somehow that comforts me.
To know that he gets nervous and flustered too.
I just don't know what to say.

You don't have to say anything, I say.
He walks beside me for a moment
and we are both quiet.

Where are you headed?
I'm about to say my uncle's house,
but instead I choose to be brave,
instead I say, *Home.*

XI.

It turns out Miles only lives a few blocks away from
    Uncle Mazin and Aunt Michelle's house.
    He invites me to stop by to meet Sputnik
    and even though I want nothing more
    than to go home
    and curl up in bed
    and pull the blankets over me and
    pretend I'm back home in my old
    sunny bedroom that smelled like jasmine and sea salt,
    I agree because I really do
    want to meet this dog.

    Sputnik is already outside when I get there,
    running around in the fenced yard.
    Miles opens the creaky wooden gate to let us in
    and Sputnik instantly runs to him,
    jumping up and licking his face.

    Down, girl, he says,
    but he laughs,

actually laughs,
as he halfheartedly pushes her back toward the ground
that is still covered with frozen leaves.

His laugh sounds like a
joyous rattle.
I would like to listen to it again
and again.

We take turns throwing the ball to Sputnik
and talking about simple things like
when our next math quiz is
and whether we think Mrs. Bloom is happy
with the way the play is turning out,
and then Miles says,

I just want to say,
and it's not that I'm saying I understand
because I know I don't,
but I do understand what it's like to not fit in.
To have people look at you like you're different
and weird
and like that's somehow a bad thing.

He stares at his black combat boots
and throws the tennis ball again for Sputnik.
It's not a bad thing, he finally says,

you know?

I nod,
his words drape over me,
feeling like the relief of
an umbrella in a storm,
the comfort of a soft blanket
on a chilly night.

I pick the tennis ball up off the cold ground,
and Sputnik runs over to me with excitement
and begins to lick my hands,
her tongue rough against my skin.

I laugh, surprised by the feel of her tongue,
surprised by all of it.

XII.

Why do they blame us? I ask Layla,
     a few days after the news of the attack,
     when we are sitting in one
     of the back rows of the theater.

     Layla gives me the shrug
     the American one,
     the one I learned from her,
     the one when you don't know the answer
     but can't quite bring yourself to admit it.
     Or maybe sometimes you shrug
     because you do know the answer,
     but it is too painful
     to say.

     Don't they know we hate this too?
     That we suffer too?
     It's only after I say it that I realize Layla
     is no longer my "we."
     She was not raised in a part of the world

where it is no longer shocking to hear
about bombs going off in
cars
markets
mosques.

Bombs going off while people are
praying
celebrating
loving.

I ask why this attack in particular is
so upsetting to Americans.
Why not last week in Lebanon?
Or the week before in Pakistan?

Layla tells me it is because this
attack
took place in the West.

She tells me Americans expect bombs to go off in
Lebanon
in Pakistan
in my beloved Syria,
but not in France,
Britain,
Canada.

She tries to explain that it is like how we all expect it to
be snowy in Antarctica
but sunny and warm in Tahiti
but if it snowed in Tahiti that would be news
because it would be unexpected,
but no one bats an eye when snow falls in
frozen Antarctica.

It takes me a while to process this,
that what Layla is saying is that Americans
think it's normal
for there to be violence
in places where
people like me are from,
where people like me
and people who look like me
live.

That they all see people like me
and think
violence
sadness
war.

That's not true, I say.
Syria wasn't always like how it is now,
and it won't always be like that either.

I feel like my brother when I say that,
his courage
his belief
his strength
echoing in my words.

For a moment,
it does not feel like Issa is missing
all the way across the world,
but instead,
sitting in this theater next to me,
giving me strength.

It is these moments when I miss him
the most.
I wonder if wherever he is,
if he is thinking about me,
about Mama and her swollen belly,
about Baba all alone at his store.

When I was younger
and I used to get upset,
Issa would say to me:
Too much sunshine makes a desert.

I wonder, though,
if it is possible for there

to be too much rain.
I am starting to feel like
I am drowning,
like I don't know how much longer
I can stay afloat.

XIII.

I am walking home from school with Miles
    when I see it.

Terrorists.

The red paint glistens in the winter sunlight like jewels,
like blood.
It is splashed across
the storefront of Layla's parents' restaurant.

I do not realize I have bent over,
am clutching my stomach,
until Miles says,
What's wrong?

His eyes follow mine
and then he sees the awful paint.

He shakes his head angrily,
his eyes hard.
Whoever did that is an awful person.

Whoever did that is a terrorist, I say,
and then bite my tongue so hard I can taste blood.

I look back at the bright red paint.
T e r r o r i s t s.

My vision blurs with tears.
For the first time since I've been in America,
I wish I didn't read English.

XIV.

I tell Mama
    what has happened.

    She pretends to receive
    the news calmly,
    but she forgets that
    her eyes speak.

    They show her
    anger and her fear.

    She pulls me into a hug
    and rubs small circles on
    my back.

    Why do they hate us?
    I ask, my voice
    foggy with tears.

    Jude.

Her tone is sharp.
I straighten my posture.
This is not about you.
It is about one person's
ignorance and fear.

It feels like
it's about me.
I feel like it's
about all of us, I say.

She rubs my
back again.
There is something
so comforting
about the infinite
nature of circles.

We need to be strong for Layla.

I know she is right.
I also know that she means
I need to be strong for her.
For me.

I miss Issa.
He would know what to do.

Mama takes a deep breath.
*Your brother would
let his anger guide him.
You are more level-headed.
That will help you
better navigate
situations like this.
You are strong too, Jude.*

Sometimes talking
to Mama reminds me
of a feather duster brushing dirt
away from a mirror.
She doesn't give you anything new,
but she helps you better see
what is already there.

What can we do? I ask,
and I am asking not only
about how we can help
Layla and her family,
but how we can continue
to live in this world
where we don't even know
if my brother is safe.

We'll figure it out,

Mama says to me,
squeezing my hand.
Together.

XV.

I try to talk to Layla,
     but she does not want to talk about it.

     Forget it, Jude, she snaps.

     I only want to help.
I am standing
in the entrance
of her parents' restaurant.
They are paying someone to scrub off the paint,
but I am slowly realizing that no amount of money
is enough to scrub away the hate.

I sit down in the front booth
and she reluctantly sits down in front of me.
You're lucky, Jude.
Please don't start that again, I say.

No, she says.
Her voice has the force of a windstorm.
You belong somewhere.

I don't belong anywhere.
Not here,
not there.

That's not true, I say,
but my voice is weak, like a gasp of air.
I want to tell her that what she's saying isn't true,
but I can tell that she doesn't want me to say anything.
She is asking simple questions
with hard answers.
All she wants is for me to
listen.

In my months of speaking English
while still thinking,
still dreaming,
in Arabic,
I have learned that sometimes
the simplest things are
the hardest things to say.
That sometimes there is no word
for what you feel,
no word in any language.

Here, I'll always look like the guy
who did it,
or look like someone the guy who did it loves, Layla says.

I can feel her drifting from me
and I want to pull her back,
but I don't know how.
She is drawing a line between us
that does not need to be drawn.

But if I go there, she finally says,
I'll always be the American.
So you see,
I don't belong anywhere.

You have me, I say.

Until you leave.

Those three words
pierce
us both.

I shake my head,
and then I do what she expects me to do.
I leave.

XVI.

Layla doesn't talk to me the next week.

Not at school in the hallway
when I see her standing by her locker
with her friend Kate talking about
their upcoming quiz in science.

Not at play practice
where she sits with Ruth
and the other set designers
and pretends I'm not there
when I walk right up to her.

Whenever I approach her,
she turns away.
I try to pretend like it doesn't bother me.
I focus on memorizing my two and a half lines
over and over again.

I focus on getting into the role of a feather duster

who has a crush on a candlestick
who sometimes notices she exists
and sometimes doesn't.

There are parts of her character
I cannot relate to.
I am not flirty and confident in the way she is,
but I try to pretend to be.

I work on understanding her better by leaning
into the parts of her
that I do understand—
the desire to be seen,
to be noticed,
to be heard.

As I pretend to have Plumette's confidence,
as I put my hand on my hip and jut it out,
I glance around to see if Layla sees me,
but whenever I look in her direction,
she isn't looking back.

XVII.

Are you nervous?
 Grace asks me.
 We are having what Mrs. Ravenswood
 calls a free chat
 where we all talk about
 anything we want.
 The only rule is
 we have to say everything
 in English.

 I'd be terrified.
 She smiles and I can tell
 she is proud of the big
 English word she just used.

 I like the word
 terrified.
 Not because of what it means,
 but because it actually feels like
 the word it is.

When you say it,
you hear the terror.
Taste it.

I shake my head and say,
I'm excited,
even though I am nervous
about the play.

I'm nervous about forgetting
my two and a half lines.
I'm nervous about messing up
in front of everyone,
about letting Mrs. Bloom down,
about giving everyone a reason
to think she was wrong to give me a role.

I'm excited, too! Grace says.
We're all going to come
see you.

She glances over at Ben and Omar
who are busy talking
about the arcade games
at the pizzeria nearby our school
where Omar has been going
with some new friends

and is trying to convince Ben
to come along.

They're coming, too, Grace says
when she can't get their attention.

Are you sure?

She smiles a little.
They said they would.
Omar said it better
not be boring.

At this,
Ben and Omar snap
to attention.

It's not going to be
boring. Right, Jude?
It's going to be dope.

Dope? I say,
trying out another
new word.

Dope means
something amazing.

Something really cool, Ben explains.

Mrs. Ravenswood
speaks for the first
time in a long time.
*Care to tell us something
else you find to be dope?*

Hearing Mrs. Ravenswood
say that word
makes us all smile.

*The Duck Hunt
game at Mario's,* Omar says.

Music, Grace says.

Any type in particular?
Mrs. Ravenswood asks.

Grace's face flushes
red and she whispers,
Rock and roll.

Really? I ask Grace.

Her face is still red,

but she nods.
She starts to rattle off the names
of American bands
I have never heard of.

That's dope, Grace,
Ben says,
and we all laugh.

I like how in Mrs. Ravenswood's room,
we are still always learning,
not only words,
but also about each other.

XVIII.

We are practicing
    one of the big group numbers
    where almost the entire cast
    including the chorus
    is on stage.

    I find these scenes
    the hardest because
    my feet have to move
    in the same direction
    as everyone's
    at the exact same time.

    I am trying to remember
    the next step of the dance
    when I look out
    and see Layla in the back
    of the theater,
    her head bent down,
    studying the artwork
    on one of the sets.

Before I realize
what is happening,
my elbow is colliding
with Thomas,
who is playing Lumiere,
who bumps into
Nathan,
who is playing Cogsworth.

Soon,
the stage is a mess
of tangled ankles
and bumped knees.

Mrs. Bloom
calls out to us.
Let's take a
short break
and regroup in
five.

My face feels
like it is on fire.
I run off the stage
and quickly escape
into the hall.

Hey, I hear a familiar voice call out.

When I turn around,
I see Miles.

Is everything okay?
he asks, and I shake my head.
Want to go outside
for a minute?

We walk down
the hallway,
push open the door,
and step into the
cool night air.

I shiver a little
and look up at the sky.
It is a clear night
and I can see a smattering
of stars.

Did you know
that when we see
a star,
we are really seeing
a past version of it
because the light
is traveling from so far away?

Miles's head is tilted up.
So looking at the stars,
in a way,
is like looking into the past.

I wish I could look
into the future, I say quietly.

What would you want to see?

My brother, I say.
I see my breath in front of me,
floating in the cold, cold air.

What do you want to know about him?

That he's okay, I say.
That he's alive.
And then it spills out of me.
I tell Miles all about Issa
and how he has run away to Aleppo
to help all those people who
are stuck in a war-torn city.
How he has become one of
those people who are stuck
in a war-torn city.

Layla is the only person
at school who I've told, I tell him.
And now you.

We are silent
for a while.
It is not a bad silence though.

Instead it feels
right
like it is acknowledging
the heaviness of what was said,
and it's okay that we don't know
what to say.

Thank you for telling me.
I really hope he is safe.

Miles points up at the sky.
Do you see that
constellation?
That's Orion.
In ancient Greek mythology,
Orion was thought to have
superhuman strength.
Basically indestructible.
Maybe it's

a positive sign that
we can see Orion clearly tonight.

I follow Miles's
finger to the collection of
twinkling stars.
A message to us
from the future?

Miles smiles a little.
That's one way to
think about it.

XIX.

One night after dinner,
    I find Uncle Mazin in his study.

    I knock on the door
    and he welcomes me in.

    Why do they hate us? I ask him in Arabic,
    almost daring him to join me in this language,
    this language that I wonder sometimes if he
    even remembers.

    It was one ignorant person, Jude,
    he says, and his Arabic is confident
    and clear.
    It is terrible what they did,
    but you can't let their hateful act
    define all of America.

    He gives me a big hug,
    and it is unexpected because my baba is not

one for big hugs and so I assumed my uncle would be
the same way.

He kisses the top of my head.
You belong here.
And so do I.

The kiss lingers on the top of my head
like a ghost
like a promise.

I belong back home, too.

He gives me a smile,
one that says,
I know.
It's not a contest between here
and there.
You don't have to choose.

XX.

The postcard comes at just the right moment.
    It is the type of thing that makes me believe in Allah
    and the grace of the universe.

    Mama hands it to me,
    tears in her eyes.

    It is a small postcard
    with a simple photograph of Beirut on the front.
    In typical Fatima fashion,
    she has not written much,
    but she has written and that is what matters.

    She is still my friend and that is what matters.

    I spend a lot of time tracing the address on the back of
    the postcard.
    I now have a way to write to her
    again.

    I feel so much less lonely.

XXI.

Mama beams with pride
　　and puts her hands on her belly that is now so big
　　it seems like it could pop
　　at any moment.

　　She has realized her wish of getting Uncle Mazin
　　to come to mosque.
　　And Aunt Michelle and Sarah are here too.
　　There are so many people here.
　　All because Mama
　　and a few of her friends from the mosque
　　have organized a fund raiser for Layla's parents
　　to help them offset the costs
　　of the damage
　　to their restaurant,
　　to help them heal.

　　People are bidding on baskets my mama put together.
　　The baskets filled with homemade ma'amoul
　　and soaps made with olive oil
　　and little bottles filled with rosewater perfume.

I make my way through the crowded room,
sipping sugary tea out of a Styrofoam cup.
I find Layla sitting near the back of the room
with a few of her friends from mosque
who don't go to our school.

At first, I think she will ignore me
like she has done for the last few weeks
at school.

But when she stands up
when she sees me
and waves me over,
I flood with relief.

Jude, she says,
smiles,
and gives me a hug.

This was so nice of your mom.
I return her smile.
She cares about you.
I care about you, I say.

Layla looks at the shiny tiled floor.
I know. I'm sorry.
It's just I was so angry.

I get it, I say,
practicing an American phrase
I have recently learned.

Your cousin seems to be
having fun.
I follow Layla's eyes
to where Sarah is standing
in a circle with some
of Mama's friends from mosque,
eating a pistachio ma'amoul
and laughing.

Wow, I say.

You sound like such an American
when you say that, Layla laughs.
We both keep watching Sarah.
She is practicing how to
say *tay'ebeh,*
delicious.

All of a sudden,
Layla reaches out and touches my shoulder.
Jude, you're brave.
You know that, right?

301

When she says that,
pressure builds behind my eyes,
and I worry I might cry
because hearing that makes me miss Issa
so
so
much.

What is it? she says.
Are you mad?

I shake my head and
blink away my tears.
I tell her I was thinking of Issa.
She squeezes my shoulder again.

He's going to be okay,
and he would be so proud of you.
Her eyes wander the room
and find Mama, who is surrounded by lots of friends.
New friends,
American friends.

He'd be so proud of all of you.

XXII.

After the fund raiser,
    Uncle Mazin
    Aunt Michelle
    Sarah
    Mama
    and I all go home.

Mama collapses into bed,
so tired,
but I stay up with the rest of my family.

Uncle Mazin is smiling more than I have seen him
smile in a while.
At the fundraiser, he met
a nurse from Jordan,
a store owner from Egypt,
a data scientist from Syria.
It felt good to talk about home with people who understood,
he says to me in Arabic.

Home.

I am surprised to hear him call Syria home.
I am happy that now Uncle Mazin and I both call this
creaky old house
and Syria
home.

We all watch a movie on TV
and when it is over
I head upstairs,
but Sarah stops me.

Jude, she says.
She invites me to her room.
The whole time I have lived here,
I have only been inside her room one other time.

Sarah laces her hands together
and rocks back and forth on the balls of her feet.
I can tell she is nervous,
but I don't know why.

I'm sorry about what I said about Layla, Sarah says.

I purse my lips together,
unsure what to say.

I remember how upset
I was when Sarah insulted Layla.
I remember how weak I felt
for not standing up to her then.
But I also remember how Mama
says that the fact I can control
my anger doesn't make me weak,
that sometimes it even makes me strong.

It's really awful
what happened to her parents' restaurant, Sarah adds.
Will you let me know if
there is anything I can do to help?

I think again
of that proverb:
She cannot give what she doesn't have.

Sarah gained something tonight.
Something she didn't have before.
And now she is giving some of it
to me.

I will, I say
with a small smile.

PART SIX
Living

I.

In Mrs. Ravenswood's class,
    we are celebrating the fact that Ben and his family
    have all become American citizens.

    Ben has brought in pictures from the ceremony
    that happened down at the courthouse.
    We drank pink lemonade, Ben says.
    And ate cookies.

    That sounds like
    the perfect celebration, Mrs. Ravenswood says
    as she passes out chocolate-chip cookies
    she bought at the grocery store
    so that we can celebrate in class too.

    Ben continues to talk about how
    his father smiled at him
    when he finished reciting the Pledge of Allegiance
    because it was Ben
    who helped his father memorize it.

After the cookies,
we go back to practicing the past tense.
Grace and I are partners,
going back and forth saying,
I ran
you ran
she ran
we ran
they ran.

That one's easy, Grace says, laughing.
It's always ran.

Maybe it's all getting easier, I say
and brush some cookie crumbs away.

II.

I am at play practice,
    watching Miles fiddle
    with a Rubik's cube.

We are sitting beside Layla
who is putting the finishing touches
on one of the set murals
that depicts the French countryside.
It is beautiful and I tell her so,
but I am also trying to tell her,

You belong here.
You make beautiful things.

Sarah sees Uncle Mazin before I do.
I hear her say,
Dad?
What are you doing here?
He gives his daughter a hug, but his eyes
are searching for me.

Khalo? I say.
She's coming, he says,
and my body breaks open like a shaken-up
soda can,
my insides fizzing,
anticipation and excitement rising to the top
and foaming over.

We go outside to get into Uncle Mazin's car
and fat snowflakes are falling from the sky.
Sarah squeezes my hand as she sits
with me in the backseat.

You're going to be a big sister! she says.
Can you believe it?

I laugh nervously
and look out the window.
As we drive to the hospital where
Uncle Mazin works and my baby sister will be
born, I think,

You will belong here.
You will belong wherever you want.
You will make anywhere beautiful.

III.

She has Baba's eyes
    and it is too early to know if she has Mama's nose
    or Baba's,
    if she has my eyebrows
    or Issa's.

When I hold her for the first time
my heart feels like it is going
to burst.
I didn't know it was possible
to love one tiny person
so, so much.

She is red and loud,
and cries at all times of the day
and night.
She makes Baba cry when he sees her
through the computer,
his arms aching to hold her.

The baby keeps her hands balled in tiny fists
like she is ready to fight
and her mouth gapes open when she sleeps,
tiny drops of drool pooling out,
but even though she is wrinkly
and drooly
and red,
she is the most beautiful thing
I have ever seen.

Mama names her Amal,
after Auntie Amal,
after hope.

IV.

Aunt Michelle never stops
    cooing over Amal.
    Even Sarah seems
    to have fallen in love
    with her.

She's so pretty, Sarah says.
I think she looks like
you
Dad
and me.

You think we look alike?
I ask, trying to mask my surprise.

Yeah, she says.
Of course.
We're cousins.

I don't even bother
to try and hide my smile.

We all take turns rocking Amal,
changing her.
Every tiny thing she does—
yawn,
squirm,
kick,
brings us so much joy.

V.

Amal has been here two weeks
    five days
    eight hours
    and Issa still hasn't seen her
    through the computer screen.
    He does not even know he has become a big brother
    again.

The weather outside has changed from snowy
    to rainy
    from sunny
    to cloudy.
    People say that spring is near,
    but all I see so far is
    mud.

Mama calls Baba all the time so he can see Amal
    when she is sleepy and snuggly
    when she is yelling her little head off
    when she is looking all around,
    wide-eyed and dazed.

317

I listen to Mama and Baba speculate
about what Amal will be like when she gets older.
Did you see her do this, do that?
they say, noticing her every move,
every tense of her back,
every shake of her head.
I wonder what they said about me,
about Issa,
when we were this little,
when we were still a
mystery,
a wonder to wonder
about.

VI.

I bring in pictures of Amal
    to show off in Mrs. Ravenswood's class.

She's so beautiful, Grace says.
She has your nose, Mrs. Ravenswood says.
She's so little, Omar says,
and we all laugh because it's such an Omar thing
to state the obvious.

When it's Ben's turn,
he looks at the photograph.
She's an American, he says,
and that's awesome.

It makes us all smile.

VII.

When Mama
    rushes down the stairs
    to find me working on my math homework,
    and I see her face,
    I start to cry before she says anything.

Taali, she says,
    motioning for me to follow her.
    She cradles Amal in her arms,
    gently singing an Arabic lullaby to her,
    to me.
    Every bone in my body
    is standing at attention
    as I follow her up the stairs.

We go into Uncle Mazin's study
    and that's when I see my brother's image.
    The blinds are pulled shut,
    the room dark,
    but my brother's face,

his smile,
is bright enough to illuminate everything.

I let out a yelp of joy.
Of relief.

Jude, he says. *You've grown up!*
Tears glisten in my eyes
as I realize he has not seen me since
I started to cover my hair.
And the baby, she's so beautiful, he says.
You're all so beautiful.

This is Amal, Mama says.
Motasharefatun bema'refatek, Amal, Issa says,
and his dark eyes smile with love for her,
for all of us.

In Issa's face,
I can see the months that have passed.
There are shadows under his eyes
that I have never seen before,
and I can make out the outline
of a bruise around his elbow.
There is unshaved scruff on his chin
and he looks much thinner.
Yet, his smile is still the same.

Bright enough to light up
the entire room.

My tears turn to laughter
and I run to the computer screen
and talk as fast as I can,
scared that if I don't say every word I know,
I think,
he will disappear.

I ask him, *Where are you?*
How have you been?
Are you going to go home?
Are you going to come here?
Can you believe I'm a big sister now?
That I'm no longer your littlest sister?

S
L
O
W
D
O
W
N
he tells me, laughing.
He has left the most dangerous place

and is in a nearby town.
He is using an international aid worker's computer to
    call us.

Despite Mama's begging,
he will not promise not to go back to the danger,
to the war zone.

I am needed there, he says,
and both Mama and my heart say,
We need you here.

But somehow, despite the fact
my brother has been in places where bombs have
dropped,
are dropping,
in places where buildings have been reduced
to ashy crumble
in places with no food
and no water,
he seems more at peace
than I have ever seen him.

You're doing It, I say,
and he says the same thing back to me,
and I'm not sure either of us really knows what
the It is, but we are okay with trying to figure it out.

We are okay with still learning our lines
because we are liking the script—
maybe, just maybe, we have both finally found roles
that make sense to us.

Roles where we feel seen
as we truly are.

I just wish that someday the script
will call for our roles to take place
on the same side of the Atlantic.
Where he could hold his new sister
kiss his mama
sing with me.

I don't say any of this to him,
but when I watch that star show up on his forehead
as his eyebrows draw together,
I know he knows
it.

VIII.

That morning,
    I find Miles before the first bell rings.

    My brother is okay.
    He's alive, I say,
    and I don't think I will
    ever get tired of saying those words.

    Miles's whole face
    breaks into a smile.
    He points at his T-shirt.
    I knew there was a reason
    to wear my Orion shirt today.

    I smile so hard
    my face hurts.
    That's one way
    to think about it.

IX.

Mama constantly talks about how Baba and Issa
  need to come to America to join us.

But it is so much harder now to come
than it was even when we came,
Mama tells me as she nurses Amal
who seems to always be hungry.

I tell Mama not to worry
that Baba knows how to take care of himself
and that Issa will be fine.
That he is going to save lives
that he is standing up for what he believes
that we should be proud of him.

She says, *Jude, when are you going to learn*
that your brother is not a superhero?
I didn't even know that Mama knew
what a superhero was
but we have been living in America now

for almost nine months.
I guess I am not the only one who has been learning
new words.

Let's have hope, is all I say,
and we both look at baby Amal,
our tiny,
tiniest,
hope,
who at that very moment,
flashes open her eyes,
and cries with hunger.

X.

We have our final practice
    before opening night.

    At the end of it,
    we all take our pretend bow,
    imagining the audience that will be
    seated there tomorrow night clapping,
    clapping for us.

    And then Mrs. Bloom does clap.
    She claps for us.
    I'm so proud of all of you, she says.
    You've worked so hard and you've brought this story
    to life.

    We all look at each other
    and clap and bow.
    Proud of each other,
    proud of what we have created
    together.

It is lovely
to be a part of something
that feels bigger than you.

XI.

It is decided that Mama will come on opening night
    and Aunt Michelle will watch Amal
    and then the next night,
    Mama will stay home and Aunt Michelle will go.

Uncle Mazin insists he can watch the baby,
but both Mama and Aunt Michelle ignore him.
I have never seen them so in sync.

I put on my costume and Mama does not comment
on the tight black leggings
or the long-sleeved patterned leotard.
As long as you are comfortable with it,
her eyes seem to say.
She has French braided my hair
underneath my hijab.
No one else will see it,
but it helps me to feel in character.
It is a secret between Mama and me,
It feels like a hidden charm
that will give me courage.

Before we leave,
Aunt Michelle takes a picture of Sarah and me.
Sarah in her chorus costume,
me in my Plumette one.

We're going to be fantastic tonight, Sarah says,
and her use of *we're,*
a contraction that I have practiced over and over
in Mrs. Ravenswood's class
feels like a tiny present to me
that I am so happy to unwrap.

We are all nervously waiting
behind the curtain.
I see Layla carefully checking the sets,
a clipboard in hand,
making notes.
Her eyes briefly meet mine
and we share a smile,
each wishing the other good luck.

I know Miles is up in the tech booth,
getting the lights ready.
The more I get to know him,
the more I appreciate how he likes
to help other people
shine.
I listen to the opening number from backstage

and my heart thunders in my chest.
The audience claps with furious delight.

The next scenes go by
and it is almost my moment,
almost my time to step out on stage,
to be seen.

I hold my breath.

The curtain lifts
and I step out onto the stage.

The theater lights are brighter than
I imagined.

I squint a little,
but then I adjust to the spotlight.

Glossary of Arabic Words

a'arf: I know; I'm aware

adhan: the call to prayer, also sometimes referred to as *braza'an*

akeed: of course

asroneyeh: afternoon snack

bint: girl

ghadah: the big family meal of the day, usually lunch

habibti: sweetheart

jebneh: cheese

khalo: uncle (on the maternal side)

mahzozeen: lucky

marhaba: hello

motasharefatun bema'refatek: honored to meet you; pleasure to meet you

muezzin: the person calling for prayer (in the context of the book, Jude is referring to the speaker whose voice she hears outside her window early in the morning)

nunu: baby

skety: be quiet; don't talk

taali: come here

tay'ebeh: delicious

za'atar: Middle Eastern spice consisting of thyme and sesame seeds

Author's Note

The first inkling of the idea that would later become *Other Words for Home* came to me in fall of 2013 when I was invited over to a close family friend's house for dinner. At this dinner, I was introduced to members of their extended family who had recently come over from Syria to escape the violence that was threatening their hometown. I learned more about the conflict in Syria, which, up until then, I'd only had a vague awareness of. At this dinner, I watched as cousins who were raised in America interacted with cousins who had been raised in Syria. It made me think about families—like my own (my father is from Jordan)—who live on different sides of an ocean. But I was writing another book at the time, so I tucked the idea away for later.

Flash forward to fall of 2016—the atrocities of the war in Syria had been splashed across the front pages of many American and European newspapers. More of the world was aware of what was happening, yet the silence in response to the suffering of an entire population felt deafening. Why didn't more people care? Why didn't more people want to help? These questions scared me. They made me confront things that I had long ago buried within me—knowledge of prejudice against Arabs and Arab Americans, Islamophobia, and America's often cool indifference to the suffering of brown people.

So I began to write the book. But I was writing from an analytical space, from my mind and not my heart. It wasn't until I found Jude's voice that the book was really born. I wrote Jude for my twelve-year-old self, who never saw a brown girl in a book who was proud of her family and where she came from. A brown girl with hopes and dreams of her own. I'm ashamed to admit that growing up I was much more like Jude's cousin Sarah than like Jude. Through societal conditioning, I learned to be a little afraid and a little embarrassed of my father's culture. I never was exposed to any media that told me to feel otherwise.

I wrote this book as a way to tell myself—both past and present versions—that as an Arab American girl, my dreams, hopes, and fears are as valid as anyone else's. That the Judes of the world deserve to have their stories told. I also hope that by introducing you to Jude, a magnanimous girl with a big heart and even bigger dreams, I will show that you don't need to be afraid of these children who are fleeing from a war zone. That they want the same things all of us do—love, understanding, safety, a chance at happiness.

We're in a period of human history where empathy is needed more than ever. As the mother of two little girls, I'm constantly trying to teach them the idea that no one ever grows poor from giving. That sharing what you have does not make what you have worth any less. I guess that's what this book is really about—the ever-growing need for generosity. And generosity is really just another word for love. So let's work on giving more love to others as well as to ourselves.

To learn more about the conflict in Syria and how you can help refugees like Jude, please consider checking out one of the following websites:

https://www.unicefusa.org/mission/emergencies/child
-refugees/syria-crisis

https://www.whitehelmets.org/en

https://www.doctorswithoutborders.org/what-we-do
/countries/syria

https://my.care.org/site/SPageNavigator/CARE
_SpecialDelivery.html

https://www.refugees-welcome.net

https://www.icrc.org/en/where-we-work/middle-east
/syria

Acknowledgments

Enormous and endless thanks (and every other word in both English AND Arabic for gigantic!) to:

Brenda Bowen, my magical and brilliant agent, who believed in this book from the first moment I told her about it and cheered me on through every draft. Brenda, thank you for your patience and your belief. Both made this book possible.

The entire team at Greenburger Associates, especially Wendi Gu (we miss you!), Abigail Frank (you are a life-saver!), and Stefanie Diaz (the best foreign rights agent an author could have!).

Alessandra Balzer, my incredible editor. I continually pinch myself that I am lucky enough to work with you. Thank you for all your support, for having not only the sharpest eye but also the warmest heart.

Everyone at Balzer + Bray, especially Kelsey Murphy. B+B is the kind of imprint that feels like a family and it's so lovely to be a part of it.

The whole amazing team at Harper, especially Suzanne Murphy, Andrea Pappenheimer, Kathy Faber, Kerry Moynagh, Nellie Kurtzman, Ann Dye, Vaishali Nayak, Patty Rosati, Jacquelynn Burke, and Liz Byer. And to Jenna Stempel-Lobell and Alison Donalty for the most gorgeous cover I could imagine. I'll never be done saying thank you for all your hard work.

Special thanks to Kima Jones of Jack Jones Literary.

George Wadih and Saad Samaan and everyone else who graciously shared details of their lives in Syria. Thank you to all my very thoughtful sensitivity readers.

Thank you to everyone who agreed to read this book early and whose enthusiastic feedback made me even more excited about Jude's story: Aisha Saeed, Rachel Strolle, Amanda Connor, Stephanie Appel, Sabaa Tahir, and Jason Reynolds. A special thanks to bookseller-extraordinaire Sara Grochowski, who has been such an advocate for my work from the very beginning. This is the place where I would like to thank every bookseller and librarian who places books into the hands of kids who need them. Thank you for everything you do.

Connie Smith for nurturing my love of poetry and giving me a copy of *Diving into the Wreck* when I was sixteen years old. My life was forever changed.

Writing books can be a lonely business. I'm ridiculously lucky to have so many incredible friends in the trenches with me. A few who deserve a special shout-out: Emery Lord, Kim Liggett, David Arnold, Becky Albertalli, Adam Silvera, Kristan Hoffman, Erica Kaufman, Christopher Adamson, James Chapin, and Ashley Keyser.

To steal Emery Lord's amazing phrasing, thanks also to my "civilian" friends who do not write but are equally important to my sanity—Alexandra Perrotti, Renee Sabo,

Rachel Meyers, Nicole Hall, Lane Winget, Tyler West, Elysse Winget, Ali Williams, and Kt DeLong, and everyone else who has listened to me complain about writing.

Everyone who watched my children so that I could "finish just this one page" or "reread this section one more time." In particular, Shymaa Salih, Remy Jacobs, Elsa Gonzalez, Linda Warga, Doug Warga, Kathleen Warga, Jeff Voegele, Rachel Warga, Linda L. Warga, and Annie Toops.

My family on both sides of the Atlantic. I love you all so much and feel so tremendously grateful to be the recipient of all of your support. Brandon Khader, I will never accept that your Arabic is better than mine, but I love you all the same. Mom, thank you for everything you do, especially being the world's best "Nana" and, in doing so, constantly teaching me over and over again the concept of unconditional love. Dad, this book would not have been possible without you. I am constantly inspired by your bravery and resilience. Also, thank you for teaching me all those proverbs. It makes me very sad that my Uncle Abdalla passed away before he had the chance to read this book. He was always my biggest fan, dedicated to reading every word I wrote even though English was not his native language. His generous and revolutionary spirit inspired the very heart of this story.

Gregory Scott Warga, words are my job, but they fail me when I try to thank you. You're my person. I adore you. Thank you for doing life with me, and also for always remembering to pay the electric bill, because we both know that I wouldn't.

Lillian Nour and Juniper Lee, you are the lights of my life. You are kind and gentle and loving and evidence of everything that is right about this world. Thank you for making me believe in magic again.

To every Arab and Arab American girl, I see you. You are worthy. Keep shining.

Turn the page for a sneak peek at Jasmine Warga's new novel, *The Shape of Thunder*.

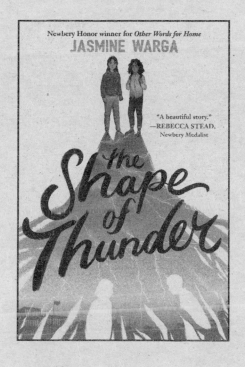

ONE
CORA

I like learning things. Especially about math and science, because they help explain why the world is the way it is. A famous mathematician once said, "Mathematics is the music of reason."

I've always believed that. The best thing about math is that it makes sense. The actual best thing about math is that everything adds up, all neat and in order.

Here's what I know about the number twelve: twelve is four times three. Twelve is six times two. Twelve is ten plus two. This is all simple math, right? Elementary-school stuff. Reason and logic. Twelve is also two less than fourteen.

Fourteen is how old Mabel was when she died.

I am twelve today. Someday in the future I will be more than twelve plus two. I will become older than my older sister.

There is no music in that fact. There is absolutely no reason. It does not add up, all neat and in order.

"You ready, Corrie?" Dad asks as he slips on his navy windbreaker. Grams is standing beside him in her puffy red coat. It's not even that cold outside, and she's been wearing it for ten minutes already. Grams is always ready before everyone else.

"We really don't have to go."

"Of course we do." Dad gives me a smile and I know it's supposed to look encouraging, but I can see the sadness leaking out behind it.

"Don't be silly," Grams says, draping an arm around my shoulder and pulling me close enough to her that I can smell her hair that always smells like lemons. Grams is the only person I know who washes their hair with a bar of soap instead of shampoo. "We always go to Pete's."

This is true. Going to Pete's for birthdays has been a Hamed family tradition for as long as I can remember. We go—all four of us—Grams, Dad, Mabel, and me. We sit in the same back corner booth—the one with saggy cushions—and order chocolate milkshakes and an extra-large pizza. Whoever's birthday it is gets to pick the pizza toppings.

For Mabel's, we'd always get barbecue chicken. Dad usually picks veggie, though I think he only does that because he's always trying to get everyone to eat more vegetables. (When Mabel and I were younger, he printed off a copy of a nutrition guide, circled the vegetable and fruits section, and hung it up on our wall—Mabel let it stay for a day, before ripping it down and replacing it with a picture of a rainbow she'd drawn at school.) Grams usually chooses whatever the monthly special is, and me? I pick cheese. Mabel used to say that cheese was boring, and well, the truth is, I'm a little bit boring.

Boring is okay with me. Boring is safe. Boring is your sister coming home from school like you expect her to.

"What's this?" Grams says. She's been idling on the porch, whereas Dad and I have already made it halfway down the driveway to where Dad's car is parked. She picks up a cardboard box. There's a thick piece of duct tape running diagonally across it to keep it shut. "Sweet pea, it has your name on it. Must be a birthday present."

I give her a confused look. There's no one besides Grams or Dad who would get me a birthday present. Maybe Owen. My stomach flips a little at that thought and then I feel guilty. Now, of all times, it's not right for my body to be doing the new fizzy thing it does when I think of him.

Grams studies the box, holding it out toward me. I know exactly who the box is from the moment I see the chunky handwriting that slopes to the left. A sticky knot forms in my throat.

Grams must recognize the handwriting too because she says, "Oh, it's from Quinn. Did you invite her to come with

3

us to Pete's?" Grams asks. She casts a quick glance toward Quinn's house, which is right next door, like it has always been, even though I've spent the last ten months trying to pretend like it doesn't exist.

I shake my head. I can't bring myself to say words. Grams should know I didn't invite Quinn. I haven't talked to her since that day.

The day Mabel died. November 11.

Dad clears his throat. "You could've invited her."

I know I'm about to get another big lecture from Dad and Grams about how I should still be friends with Quinn McCauley. The conversation always goes the same way: they tell me that I shouldn't hold what Quinn's brother did against her, that Mabel wouldn't want me to punish Quinn.

The thing is, though, deep down, I think Mabel would hold a grudge against Quinn, and she'd expect me to, too.

It's not that my sister was mean or anything, but she was what grown-ups call "a force." When she got mad, she stayed mad. Even about silly, stupid things. She never forgave David Wilkes for breaking the ceramic bird she made in second grade, and she never forgave Addison Taylor for wearing the exact same red glittery dress as her to the eighth-grade end-of-the-year dance.

Mabel wasn't always nice. She got mad a lot. Those two things are facts. You simply can't argue with them.

That's one of the things I hate the most about Mabel

being gone. People want to remember her differently, perfectly. She was Mabel, my sister, my favorite person in the whole world, but she wasn't perfect. I want to remember her as she was. My memory of my sister is a triangle, made up of bold lines but also sharp angles, and everyone else wants to remember her as a boring and simple circle.

I open the car door and slide into the back seat. Grams holds on to the package from Quinn, cradling it in her lap, as Dad steers the car out of the driveway. I keep sneaking glances at the box, wondering what could possibly be inside, even though I don't want to be thinking about it.

I don't want to be thinking about the McCauley family at all.

Outside the car window, the sun is hanging low in the sky, about to slip below the horizon, and it's making a hazy orange trail. We drive by tree-lined streets and manicured postage stamp–sized lawns where leaves have been raked into neat piles by the curb.

September, my birthday month. It used to mean new school supplies, freshly sharpened pencils and blank notebooks. School used to be a place that was safe. A place where I learned things. But last year, I learned the worst thing: no place is really safe.

So these days when I think of September, I think of it as the time of year when night starts earlier and lasts longer—a darkness that comes and doesn't leave.

Dad steers the car along the road that will lead us to

downtown. Chestnut, my hometown, is one of a collection of small Ohio towns that are along the old railway line, which means we have a little downtown-type square. It's mostly shops and restaurants with one hardware store, and also a new fancy pet food place that just came in. Grams thinks the pet food place is wild. "People are feeding their dogs more expensive food than I eat!" she says, but the store always seems to be crowded. That's Chestnut for you.

Pete's Pizza is in this downtown square. Dad parks the car and we all get out. He holds the restaurant door open for Grams and me. When I walk through, he says, "Twelve. I can't believe my little girl is twelve. I'm probably going to have to stop calling you my little girl soon, huh?"

I blink the tears away from my eyes before Dad can see them. I have to be strong for him.

I'm the only Hamed girl left.

Dad gently presses his hand into the small of my back. As we walk toward the booth, I look over my shoulder. I spot our car in the front row of the parking lot. In the passenger seat, I can make out the shadowy outline of the cardboard box. The fading sunlight hits it in a way that makes it look like it's winking at me.

I take a deep breath and turn my head away.

TWO
QUINN

Dear Parker,

I only ever saw you cry once.

It was in the woods. It was after you helped me down from the tree.

Do you remember?

Dad always told us not to cry. Especially you.

The time I saw you cry, it wasn't because you were sad.

I haven't cried since it happened, but I'm pretty sure I'm going to cry when I see you again.

Your sister,
Quinn

It's been three days since I put the box on Cora's doorstep, and I still haven't heard anything from her.

The last bell of the day rings, and I jolt toward the library. As I scramble to get there before anyone spots me, I imagine the scene being narrated by one of those voices from the boring documentaries we sometimes watch at school. The kind of voice that speaks in a stiff and funny-sounding way, like: *Quinn McCauley races down the tiled halls in the hopes that none of her classmates will notice her before she has once again disappeared from view.*

"Hi, Quinn," Mrs. Euclid greets me as I walk into the library.

Before last year, I hardly ever went to the school library. Maybe because I've never thought of myself as a great reader or Language Arts student. Whenever I get one of my writing assignments back, there's so much red on it, circling all the things I did wrong, that it looks like it's bleeding. I mean, I think I have okay ideas. But I'm never able to get them down without lots of spelling and grammar mistakes or something else wrong.

I lose track of my thoughts a lot. I have so many of them that by the time it comes to write them down, it ends up coming out all wrong, and my teachers start to think I don't have any thoughts at all.

I'm also never able to memorize facts from books, so I sometimes do badly on reading quizzes. I mean, I could tell you why I liked the book. Or why I didn't. Or how I felt about the characters. But my teachers always want to know things like what color glasses the main character wore and those are the types of details that slip my mind. Those are also the type of details my brain forgets when I get nervous. And I'm always nervous during quizzes.

Anyway, I didn't think the library was for me. I figured it was only for kids like Cora who are really good at school.

But after last November, I started coming in here all the time. And when school started back up this year, I found myself here again. I've figured out that I kinda love the library. The long line of shelves, the quiet hum of the ceiling fan, and the smell. The library totally smells a certain way. Kind of musty, but also welcoming. It smells like a place where you can belong.

I sit down at a table in the back, and Mrs. Euclid pushes a cart of books toward me.

"We just got a book in that I think you'll like."

"Really?"

Mrs. Euclid smiles, and I notice her bright-colored purple lipstick. Mrs. Euclid is Black and wears her hair in long box braids that almost reach her waist. Today she has on earrings shaped like BB-8 and her shoes are ballet flats that look like mice. Mrs. Euclid always has the best shoes.

"It's on your favorite topic. Time travel!" She reaches down and fishes a book off the cart. She hands it to me.

9

The cover has a boy standing in the middle of a light tunnel.

"He travels all the way back to the Jurassic era. Pretty cool, huh?"

I turn the book over in my hands. I stare at the boy on the cover, and irritation itches inside me. This boy did what I want to do. Also, for some reason, it's almost always a boy on these type of books. Super annoying.

I point at the cover. "Isn't that kind of a spoiler?"

"How so?"

"Because he's standing in that light tunnel, so we already know that he managed to time-travel. Why should I read the book?"

Mrs. Euclid laughs a little. "I think the book is more about what happens after he time-travels. Not so much about whether or not he is able to."

"Hm." I'm not sure this book will be that useful for my research, but I thank Mrs. Euclid anyway.

I can hear kids talking in the hallway outside the library. Once upon a time, this was my favorite part of the day. School can be tough because it's so much sitting.

But the end of the day was great. It's when I got to see all my friends. Cora has always been my best friend, but I used to have other friends, too. Lots of them, actually. Like Scarlett and Ainsley, who I played soccer with on the weekends, and after our games, we'd beg our parents to take us out for ice cream, and then we'd have a sleepover at Ainsley's house, building massive pillow forts in her basement.

And there was Jacob and Bea and Emerson, we'd all been friends since kindergarten. Last year before it happened, I ate lunch with them every day, and then played tetherball with Bea at recess. I was always a better player than Bea, but I sometimes let her win when I knew she was having a bad day.

Now none of those kids talk to me.

They talk about me, sure.

But they don't talk to me.

It's okay, though. I even kind of actually get it. Like they can't look at me and not see what my brother did. And I mean, I can't look at me and not see what Parker did, so I don't really blame any of them. Even though I'd be lying if I said that it doesn't feel like sandpaper scratching my skin every time one of them turns away in the hall, pretending like they don't know me.

But like I said, it's okay.

It's okay because I'm going to fix it.

Mom has this lipstick that's a shade of red called "Leading Lady." Back before everything happened, when Mom still was busy with work, she would wear that lipstick. She said it was a bright spot that could get her through even the toughest and hardest of days. It was a fake-it-until-you-make-it sort of thing.

11

That's how I feel about this plan. You see, whenever I think about Parker, I end up missing him so much I feel sick. I feel sick because what kind of person misses someone who did what Parker did? And then my sickness turns to anger, an anger so hot that I feel like I could spit lava. When my anger gets that hot, I go back to thinking about my plan. And boom. Bright spot. The lava cools down.

It's actually better than a bright spot. It's a changer of spots. It's a fixer, my plan.

I call it my plan, but really it's Cora's. She's the one who has always been interested in time travel. That's how I came up with this whole thing.

One night, I was sitting at the computer, listening to Mom and Dad argue about the things that they keep promising to one another that they won't argue about in front of me (money, the guns, everything with Parker) and I didn't want to listen to them anymore, so I distracted myself by clicking on random article after random article.

Mom teases me that I turn into a zombie when I'm on the computer, clicking from one thing to another. I used to find that joke funny, but then Parker actually did become infected by things on the internet, and when I think about that, I get that lava-vomiting feeling again.

Anyway, I don't really know how I found the article. Maybe I was missing Cora, and somehow that led me there. I guess I saw the headline, and it seemed like something she might be interested in, so I clicked on it, even though I knew

I wouldn't understand all the science-y language. I clicked on it because I hoped that reading it would make me feel like I was talking to her again.

Even with all the science-y language, I was able to understand a few things. I was able to understand that a very smart scientist who worked at one of those super-famous schools, the type of school that Cora talks about wanting to go to for college, was saying that time travel was possible. He used all these other strange words like *wormholes* and *fabric of our universe* and *light speed*, but what stuck with me was the word *possible*.

Even a girl like me who doesn't understand a lot of science-y terms knows what *possible* means.

Possible means it's real.

Possible means it could happen.

I remember in fourth grade, my teacher, Mrs. Banks, told us about this old guy in ancient Greece named Archimedes who shouted "Eureka!" in the bathtub when he figured out the answer to a really tough math problem. Since I'm never the one who figures out the really tough math problem, that story was sort of lost on me, but as I read this interview with this very smart scientist, I whispered, "Eureka."

This was it.

This was the solution.

Time travel was possible, and I was going to do it. I wish I could say that I started my research that night. But I didn't. That all came later.

Instead, I ran to the corkboard in my room, where I keep old photos of Cora and me. My corkboard is a collection of things that I love. On it, I've pinned a small poster of the US women's soccer team, the menu from my favorite hamburger place, a picture of my soccer team from last year, and one of me with my mom on a beach in North Carolina when we were visiting Gammie and Papa. I used to have a photo of my whole family, but I took it down last November. I couldn't stand to look at my brother's face.

And the rest of my corkboard is filled with photos of Cora and me. Even after it happened, even after Cora stopped talking to me, I didn't take down any of the pictures. There are photos of us at all ages, including what I think is the first picture of us ever. It's from Cora's birthday party when she turned two. That was her first birthday after her mom left.

I never met her mom. Or if I did, I don't remember. I don't remember the party either, but I've always loved this picture because it proves that Cora and me go way back. I would look at it whenever I felt moody that she was spending so much time after school with the Talented and Gifted club or wasn't able to eat lunch with me because she'd been invited to a special pizza party that was only for kids who got an A on the math test. It helped remind me that she really was my best friend. My best friend since forever.

In the photo, my face is smeared with chocolate cake,

and my white freckled arms are squeezing Cora's waist. Cora's smiling perfectly for the camera, and there isn't even a speck of chocolate icing around her lips. While my striped purple shirt has sloppy brown splotches all over it, her pink dress is completely unstained. My light red hair was already long, falling in front of my face in a tangled mess. Cora's hair hadn't come in all the way yet, but you could already tell that it was going to be thick and curly like her dad's. She has his same dark olive skin tone, too. Grams has always said that Cora's golden-hazel eyes come from her mom, but I'm not sure. I just know that her and Mabel had the same eyes. Cora was always proud of that.

After last November, looking at that photo felt like pressing on a bruise. I would see it and it would remind me of everything that was lost.

But that night, after I read the article about time travel, I saw potential when I looked at that photo. I saw the word *possible*.

Maybe Cora and I had become friends for this very reason. Because we were meant to fix everything.

"Eureka," I repeated, staring at our two-year-old faces.

Books by Newbery Honor Winner
JASMINE WARGA

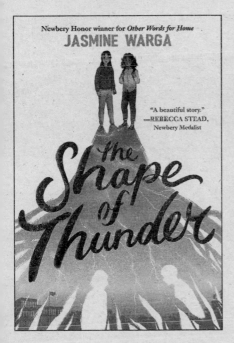

BALZER + BRAY

An Imprint of HarperCollinsPublishers

harpercollinschildrens.com